Looking for Love?

At a time when the UK Parliament is unable to agree on any government plan for Brexit a young freelance journalist, Jack Abinger, is hired to write a memorial history of an organization which for 25 years had worked to increase understanding between people in Britain and other countries of the European Union. The Journalists' European Exchange Programme had been set up by a wealthy philanthropist, in whose will provision was made for the publication of its history, JEEP having been wound up during the financial crisis of 2008.

In pursuit of his research Abinger is given the personal diaries of the man who was director of JEEP throughout its existence, and who had also recently died. The diaries add little to the information in the official records of the organization; but they gradually reveal the development of a personal relationship with a young woman member of staff which astonishes Abinger, and widens his understanding of the many meanings of 'love'.

Looking for Love?

Derek Walker

ISBN 978-1-4457-5010-1

Typesetting and design by Christine Price

Published 2021 by Derek Walker,
Dorset Square, London NW1

Distribution at www.lulu.com

ABOUT THE AUTHOR

DEREK WALKER grew up in Northern Ireland and was educated at Portadown College. He graduated at the London School of Economics, majoring in International Relations, and since then he has continued to live in London. For ten years he worked as a journalist, latterly as Deputy Editor of the *British Weekly*. In 1966 he became Education Officer of the newly-formed Voluntary Committee on Overseas Aid and Development. When VCOAD was dissolved in 1977 he became Director of the Centre for World Development Education (later renamed Worldaware) which took over its educational and public awareness-raising work. For ten years he chaired the European Development Education Curriculum Network (EDECN). In 1997 he was appointed OBE. Since retiring from Worldaware he has published nine novels (see end pages).

It was pure coincidence that the day on which I received the commission to write *A Short History of the Journalists' European Exchange Programme* was also the day on which, for the second time, Theresa May's proposals for leaving the European Union in an orderly fashion were defeated in the House of Commons. It was only later that evening, as I watched the voting on television, I reflected on how the irony of the coincidence might not have been lost on the man whose legacy was going to pay my fee. He was the late Herbert Bodley, founder of the Bodley European Educational Trust, of which the JEEP had been a subsidiary project.

The interview to confirm my appointment to the task of writing the book was with the solicitor who was one of the executors of Bodley's very considerable estate - £27 million, according to *The Times*. A balding, bespectacled man in his sixties, his name was Wilfred George; and my name had been suggested to him by one of his junior colleagues with whom I had regular consultations on copyright issues.

"Miss Mackay tells me that you work as a freelance journalist and so you will be able to start on the book straight away," he said.

"That is correct," I confirmed. "My only firm commitment at present is an article every month for the magazine *Great Captains*. So I can get into this job tomorrow morning. Is there a deadline to which you would like me to work?"

He stroked his chin thoughtfully and replied, "I think it would be desirable to publish the book while Mr Bodley's name is still fresh in people's memories. It's just two months since his death, and I wonder whether it might be possible to have the book available for distribution before next summer. It's not that many of the readers are likely to be aware of his name, because he had little personal involvement with the Exchange Programme, but he wanted it to be remembered as a distinct part of his contribution to co-operation in Europe. It's a story that is now complete, because the Exchange Programme was wound up in 2009, whereas the Bodley European Educational Trust, which funded it, will continue its work indefinitely. Mr Bodley left it very generously endowed."

"Do you know why the Journalists' Exchange Programme was discontinued?" I asked.

"It would seem that the Trust's investment income took a hit in the 2008 financial crisis, and that happened to coincide with the retirement – at the age of sixty-five – of the Exchange Programme's Director, who had set it up and been its moving spirit from the beginning. I think Mr Bodley felt that if economies had to be made the tidiest and most effective way to make them would be to end the Programme," he replied.

"Will it be possible for me to meet the former Director? He must be the person who knows more than anyone else about the Programme," I said.

"Alas, no. He died about four months ago – sudden heart attack. I think Mr Bodley had assumed that he would be the person to write the history and didn't have time to suggest an alternative before his own untimely death. His name was Winston Chatwell, and a relative of his has been in touch with us about a pension document after his death – a nephew, I think, because he didn't have any children. I still have his contact details and he might be someone you would find it useful to interview. It would seem that Chatwell was the driving force behind the Exchange Programme from beginning to end. Your other main source of information should be the remaining archive files. They're lodged at the offices of the BEET, and I'll arrange for you to have access to them.

"One other thing," he added. "The bequest makes provision for you to visit a number of the European locations where exchanges took place over the years. The funding should be enough for you to cover a sample half-dozen of them – though not travelling first class, of course."

"Of course," I responded. "That's not something I'm accustomed to. Is there any provision for visiting some of the locations in Britain?"

"Yes, that has also been provided for, although you may well find that some of the regional newspapers or radio stations involved in the scheme no longer exist, or have been merged with others."

"That wouldn't surprise me," I said. "A good reason for getting started with my research straight away could be to make sure that no more of them have disappeared before I've had a chance to speak to them."

Mr George then made out a generous advance cheque to fund the beginning of my research, and his briskly efficient PA supplied me with the name and address of Winston Chatwell's nephew, a Mr Gordon Ash, who lived in Hove.

On my way out I decided that I ought to take the opportunity to thank the colleague who had recommended me for the job, and so I took the lift to the third floor, where the department dealing with intellectual property was located. I had been a regular monthly visitor there since becoming a freelance contributor to *Great Captains* some eighteen months earlier. Although I wasn't a member of staff (there were only three full-timers) the editor had asked me to take on the task of finding illustrations, and for that I was paid a small but useful retainer. When there were technical problems about the copyright of any picture I was able to consult with the specialist solicitors with whom the group of magazines to which *Great Captains* belonged had a contract. That was how I had come into contact with my benefactor, Judith Mackay.

Luckily Judith was not with a client and the formidable receptionist, Miss Hardcastle, allowed me to go into her office. She seemed to be genuinely pleased that I had been given the job. Since her time cost the magazine money I had always been brisk and business-like in our in our monthly encounters, but this was a social call and so I was more relaxed.

I thanked her for recommending me, and she said, "I don't expect it will be a very interesting job for you, but I hope they will pay you well."

"It's a very reasonable fee for the amount of work involved," I replied, "and having my name on a second book could be useful later on, with publishers. But I'd be surprised if it has a wide readership. I think Mr Bodley wanted to be sure that there was a permanent record of what happened in the Exchange Programme; and no doubt some of the people who were involved in the scheme will be pleased to have a copy on their bookshelves."

"You never know. With all the excitement over Brexit a lot of people might become nostalgic and make your book into a bestseller, up there with *Fifty Shades of Grey*," she said, with a teasing note in her voice.

I laughed, and then, encouraged by her smile, I said, "Any chance you might be free at lunchtime? We never have time to talk properly on my monthly consultations. There's a little Italian place near here that's very pleasant – and now that I'm in the money, thanks to you, I'd be happy to treat you."

I was surprised by my own temerity and half-expected a rebuff, but she smiled and said, "Oh, what a nice idea. I don't usually go out for lunch, but I'm not particularly busy today. It will make a nice change from eating at my desk." She glanced at her watch. "It's past midday. I could come now, if that suits you."

It suited me very well, and it wasn't long before we had crossed Regent Street and made our way to Caffé Piccolo, where Giovanni found us a corner table. I was pleased to discover that Judith was also a lover of Italian food, and she was happy to select a pasta from the extensive menu.

"Who will you be writing about in the magazine next month?" Judith asked, as we waited for the food to arrive.

"Robert Blake, the man Horatio Nelson described as the greatest British naval commander of all time," I replied.

"How come I've never heard of him? I did learn some British history at school," she responded.

"Probably because he got written out of the record when the monarchy was restored. He commanded the Navy in the years when it had ceased to be 'Royal'. But in addition to beating the hitherto invincible Dutch and teaching the Barbary corsairs a lesson, he created the biggest fleet that Britain had ever had. And it was he who produced the first set of written regulations for the Navy, on which all the subsequent ones have been based. But his title wasn't admiral: he was actually called general at sea.

"Sorry. I didn't mean to launch into a history lecture," I concluded, hoping I hadn't got off to a bad start.

"Not at all," she said. "I can see now why you've chosen him as a subject."

"Did you go to school in Scotland?" I asked.

"Only to infant school," she replied. "My father moved from Edinburgh to a new job in Bristol when I was about five years old. But people say I still have traces of a Scottish accent. Do you think so."

"I thought I detected a kind of lilt that isn't English," I said. "I think the way people talk at home, in the family, can be an important influence – unless, of course, you go away to live in a boarding-school."

"I went to a day school, a very good one," she said.

"I did, too. It was co-educational, which I think has an important influence on the way you see the world, maybe particularly if you're a boy," I said.

She smiled. "Mine was a girls' school, but I have two brothers, which I think helped to keep me from getting blinkered."

"When did you graduate?" I asked, as a waiter arrived with a basket of rolls.

"Two years ago," she replied. "I was at Nottingham. Where did you go?"

"I went to Bristol. I thought it was important to move away from home, and at that time home was London. But then I came back for a year to do a Master's at the LSE. As it happens, my parents had moved to the Netherlands in the previous year. My father works for Unilever. However, that was lucky for me, because they decided to buy a small flat in London, where either or both of them can stay when they visit; and now I live there, just paying the rates and the running costs. When they do visit I use a sofa-bed in the living-room."

"That was jolly lucky for you, given the cost of living in London nowadays," she said, helping herself to a roll from the basket. "I rent a flat with two other girls, but even then it's pretty expensive. All the same, I'd rather live fairly close to work than be out in the sticks, having to commute every day."

"Where is your flat?" I asked.

"In Judd Street, not far from King's Cross. Where do you live?"

"On the top floor of a converted Georgian house, overlooking a leafy square in Marylebone. It's quite small but very pleasant. I am lucky."

Our lunch arrived at the table: ravioli for me and tortelloni for Judith. She had declined my offer of a glass of wine and we shared a bottle of sparkling mineral water.

"Do you often visit your parents?" she asked. "I've only been to Holland once, to see an exhibition in Amsterdam."

"I've been about a half-a-dozen times in the five years since they moved there. They have a house in Delft, which is a delightful place; and it's very easy to get around the country by train, and over to Belgium as well. There are so many interesting galleries to visit, and a lot of unspoilt architecture. I've really enjoyed it."

"So you're interested in art, then?" she said. "My favourite period is the Renaissance and I keep going back to Italy, but I do want to see more Northern Renaissance stuff."

I smiled. "And I want to see more Italian," I said, "but I travelled around quite a bit, in Tuscany and the Veneto."

"Did you go to Italy on your own?" I asked.

"The first time was with my parents, to Rome. Then I went with a couple of university friends to Florence. We had very little money to spend; so we learned how to live frugally. Fortunately, pasta is quite filling, especially spaghetti. Then one year I went to Venice on my own. And last year I went back to Venice with my flatmates, Henrietta and Georgina, and we travelled around quite a lot. Money's not so much of a problem now."

As I finished my ravioli I reflected that I had acquired – and given – quite a lot of useful information, should I want to take the relationship further. We had both already been to see an exhibition which had opened at the Royal Academy in the previous week, "The Nude in Renaissance Art", and that became our topic of conversation through to the arrival of coffee, Judith having declined my offer of a dessert.

She had indicated that it would not be a good idea for her to over-stay her lunch hour, and so I quickly paid the bill. As Judith stood up to put on her white raincoat, brought by the waiter, I had a moment of decision. She was, as always, neatly and soberly dressed, in a navy jacket and skirt and light blue blouse. As she turned to take the raincoat her tightly-fitting skirt emphasized the curve of her hips and what I once saw described as "hip spring" – the angle of waist to buttocks. I must have been about twelve at the time, but it has remained in my memory ever since. With Judith the angle was undoubtedly in the ideal region of forty-five degrees.

"There is so much more I'd like to talk to you about," I said. "Is there any chance you might be able to manage another lunch after we have our monthly consultation on Friday week?"

She smiled, and for the first time I observed that her eyes, behind the slight severity of her dark-rimmed spectacles, were hazel in colour.

"I'd like that," she said, "but on one condition: you must let me pay next time."

"I have no problem with that," I said, as we turned towards the door. And I felt more optimistic than I had been for a long time.

2

I spent the following day at the Bodley European Educational Trust, whose offices were on the first and second floors of an old, red-brick building in Buckingham Palace Road, very close to Victoria Station. I learned from the receptionist, a ginger-haired girl called Gloria who had been briefed to assist me, that JEEP had been located on the third floor, which was now occupied by a literary agency. She found me a table at which to sit while I sorted through some sixty files that had been retained after JEEP was closed down.

A quick skim through the annual accounts was all I needed to see that the organization had never encountered any financial problems. I made a few notes of totals that illustrated the slow and steady expansion of its activities. Personnel files revealed that there had been few staff changes in the course of its twenty-five years of existence. Winston Chatwell had been its Director from beginning to end, and there had been only one change of Finance Officer, roughly half-way through. Three different people, two women and one man, had held the post of Logistics Officer. There had also been a series of five Secretarial Assistants, all women; and the post of Personal Assistant to the Director had been held by three different women. Only one other staff title appeared in the files, that of Translator and Administrative Assistant. It had been held from November 1983 to August 1986 by a woman called Perdita Preston, and she did not seem to have had a successor.

I made some brief notes on all the staff, in the hope that some of them might still be contactable. They had all apparently been enrolled in a pension scheme, apart from Ms Preston, for whom there seemed to be no forwarding address.

The most interesting files were the three which contained the twenty-five printed annual reports. These, I presumed, would tell me most of what I needed to know for the book. Gloria was happy to let me borrow them, and I had brought with me a suitcase on wheels which made that a possibility (although the paper weighed a lot heavier than the contents I would normally carry in the suitcase when going on holiday). Well content with my first day's research, I walked to Victoria Underground station. The change at Oxford Circus to the Bakerloo Line was strenuous with the heavy suitcase, but I was pleased to have saved a taxi fare.

It wasn't until after I'd had dinner – haddock fishcakes and 'cabbage greens' – that I opened my copy of *The Times*. (Usually I read it in a morning coffee break, but on that morning I had arranged an early visit to the BEET office.) The paper contained a supplement on 'Intellectual Property', which normally I would have discarded, but I thought it might provide an opportunity for me to impress Judith with my interest in her subject at our next meeting, and so I opened it. However, I quickly discovered I was out of my depth with articles that ranged from controls on the Internet to laws affecting video games, and how Brexit might determine a European approach to brand protection. There would surely be more interesting topics for conversation; and I turned instead to the contents of *Times 2* for a little relaxation.

Next morning I began trying to telephone those former JEEP members of staff from whom there were contact numbers in the files. It proved to be a thankless task. Of the five Secretarial Assistants only one was still in the job to which she had initially moved, and she was on maternity leave. With varying degrees of suspicion in their voices the successors to the other four declined to give me a contact number. I had no better luck with two of the former Personal Assistants; but the third, who was now working for an art gallery in Mayfair, agreed to meet me in her lunch break on the following Monday. Her name was Barbara Keller and she sounded as if she would be happy to talk about her time at JEEP.

I then rang the number the solicitor had given me for Winston Chatwell's nephew, whose name was Gordon Ash. I got through to him at the second attempt, and he sounded very willing to talk to me. Although he was Chatwell's next of kin he had not had many contacts with his uncle, he said, but he would be happy to tell me anything that might be helpful. He also had some of his uncle's papers that he thought might be useful to me, and so we arranged that I should visit him on Saturday morning at his home in Hove.

Having made the phone calls I spent the rest of the day working on my article about Robert Blake. Fortunately I had done most of the necessary research at the London Library in the previous week, because for this subject the Internet was not a particularly useful source.

On Saturday morning I took the train to Brighton. When I arrived at the station I remembered the last occasion when I had gone there, about ten years earlier. I had accompanied my father to a county cricket match at Hove; and as that was where I was now heading I remembered the route, turning right as I came out of the station for a walk of about half-an-hour. On several occasions we had been to the Sussex county ground, and so the walk brought back a rush of memories. It also reminded me that it had been too long since I last telephoned my parents, and I resolved to give them a call that evening.

Gordon Ash lived in one of the pleasant suburban houses that I must have passed in my walks to and from the cricket ground. When I rang the doorbell he greeted me warmly, and his wife appeared and offered tea or coffee. I opted for tea. (I have observed that home-brewed coffee, however excellent the brand, rarely matches what a well-trained barista can produce on an Italian machine.)

"I never really got to know my uncle," said Ash, when we had settled in his drawing-room. "When I was young there was still some friction because he had married a West Indian girl and the rest of the family, including my parents, didn't approve. Nowadays it seems ridiculous, when you think about it. Very sadly, she died in an air accident after about ten years, and there was never an opportunity for reconciliation. But Uncle Winston did sometimes meet with me – and my sister, Winifred – when we were in London, and he was very kind to us. He hadn't had any children of his own, but I don't know whether that was deliberate or by accident."

"Did he marry again?" I asked.

"No. I think he lived a fairly solitary life; but of course his work at the Media Exchange Programme must have involved a great many social contacts. He told me once how much he enjoyed the travel. I think he was particularly fond of Italy, and I know he spent a lot of time there in the years after he retired. He was very interested in painting and sculpture. I've been sorting out his books and there are dozens of them on those subjects. But I didn't find the names of many personal friends in his address book. There were a few that were crossed out and I expect they were friends who had died."

"That's interesting," I said. "Of course I'll be concerned only with the time when he was running the Exchange Programme, but it's useful to have a feel for the kind of person he was. I'd like to get as much human interest as possible into the story."

"I do have something that might help you there," he said. "I discovered a box that contains a lot of diaries. They begin in the year when he took on the Exchange Programme and end about five years later. I haven't read them – not really interested – but they seem to be pretty cryptic. I just glanced at a few of the early ones and they say things like 'Committee met in morning. Useful discussion. Decided X or Y' – that kind of thing. But they might tie in with some of the official documents that I expect you've been given to look at."

"I'm sure they could be useful in that way," I replied, "especially if they record his opinion on decisions that were taken. He might not always have agreed with a committee, or with the patron of the project, whose Trust was funding it. Readers love to get a glimpse behind the official story. I'll let you have them back when I've finished my research."

"Please don't bother," said Ash. "They would only gather dust. You can throw them away when you've finished with them."

I asked if there were any relevant photographs, but he was able to produce only three. One was from his uncle's schooldays and showed what must have been a seven-a-side Rugby team of teenage lads in striped jerseys. Another was a wedding photograph, depicting a smiling Chatwell standing beside a strikingly beautiful, young, black woman. Since he had been widowed several years before becoming Director of JEEP I didn't think it would be appropriate to use that one as an illustration in the book. However, there was another picture in which Chatwell was with a group of five men and two women, who were identified in a hand-written note on the back as the JEEP Management Council. Their names were listed, and one of them was Herbert Bodley. Chatwell I could recognize from the wedding photograph, although his hair had gone distinctly grey. He seemed to be of about average height, whereas Bodley's bald head towered above the group. He must have been over six feet tall, and his expression was appropriately benevolent.

"That picture could make a useful illustration," I said. "The date on the back suggests it was taken around the time when JEEP was set up."

The diaries were heavy and Ash thoughtfully offered to give me a lift to the station, which I gratefully accepted.

As I cooked a Marks and Spencer steak and kidney pudding for my dinner that evening I reflected that, although the history I had been commissioned to write was likely to prove unexciting, I now had nearly all the raw material I needed to get started.

After I had telephoned my parents – and attempted unsuccessfully to answer their questions about Brexit – I was ready to slump in front of the television. There was nothing that I wanted to watch, but the News provided a little excitement. Although I'm not a devotee of Rugby, having had enough of it at school, there was a thrill in seeing that injury time try which enabled England to snatch a draw in the Calcutta Cup.

3

I had arranged to meet Barbara Keller on Monday at the gallery where she worked. It was situated in a quiet street on the edge of Mayfair. Since she was giving up her lunch hour to help my research I thought it would be a reasonable expense to take her to the nearby Wolseley – and I would enjoy a good lunch as well. I called for her at the gallery and we quickly crossed over Piccadilly to the restaurant.

She was a smartly-dressed woman, in her early forties I guessed (though I am sometimes mistaken when I try to estimate women's ages on first acquaintance). As we walked along we both quickly relaxed, and she told me she had been working in the gallery, in various capacities, for about ten years. "It was actually Mr Chatwell who encouraged me to go into the art business," she said. "I'd had an interest in art since I was at school, and he used to talk to me about pictures he'd seen when he was travelling on the continent."

Our conversation was interrupted by our need to study the menu and order when we arrived at the restaurant. I assumed that she might not want to be delayed and over-stay her lunch hour – but I could have been mistaken in that, because I discovered that she now had a senior position at the gallery.

As we waited for the first course to arrive I asked her how she had come to be involved with JEEP.

"I'd been in a boring job as PA to the managing director of a property company in the City," she replied. "I had a Modern Languages degree from Nottingham, but I didn't want to be a teacher and it was the only job I could find when I graduated – and after I'd taken a short secretarial course. At my interview Mr Chatwell said there would be opportunities to use my French and Italian, and I liked the idea of being involved in a European organization. In those days nobody was talking about Brexit."

"And now they seem to be talking about nothing else," I said. "Did the job involve any travel to Europe?"

"No. It was my job to hold the fort when Mr Chatwell made trips overseas. But I met a lot of visitors from the continent and that was interesting. I did my travelling in the holidays, and Mr Chatwell was very helpful with advice about where to go and what to see. When he found out I was interested in art he used to send me postcards of famous paintings from places he was visiting."

"Was he interested in art himself?" I asked.

"Yes. Very much. He used to joke that one of the perks of his job was getting to visit galleries he might not otherwise have been able to go to."

The first course arrived and conversation was suspended for a short time. Then I asked her if there had been any changes in the way in which the organization operated during the time when she was there.

"There was some discussion about possible changes," she replied. "I remember that one of the Management Council, Patricia Silverton, was very keen on extending the programme to journalists working in television. Winston – people always used his first name – did quite a lot of research on the possibility; and, of course, I typed up his report to the Council. If they've given you the Council minutes I'm sure you'll find a copy of it."

"Yes, I have all the Council minutes and I'll certainly be looking at it. Did they decide to go ahead with television?"

"No. I think the main problem was that – in those days, anyhow – making a TV programme was going to involve more than one person, and JEEP was very much geared to individuals. If I remember correctly that was the main issue, although there were some other considerations. You'll see it all in the report."

"The staff was very small, so presumably Mr Chatwell was very 'hands on' in every aspect of what you were doing," I said.

"That's right. There were just five of us, and so everybody was kept busy. But the funding remained pretty much the same, and that meant there wasn't any expansion in the number of exchanges that were handled every year. There was a settled kind of rhythm to the work."

I asked if she had met many of the European journalists who came to Britain, and she said it was mainly the Logistics Officer and Mr Chatwell who had personal contact with them. "I did meet a few of the British journalists who went to Europe," she added. "When they came back they usually looked in at the office for a kind of debriefing. Winston often took them out to lunch and invited me to join them. He said it made for a more relaxed atmosphere, and they often talked quite freely about the non-professional aspects of their experience, which he thought were very important. He used to say it wasn't just the articles that the journalists wrote, both in the paper where they were visiting and in their own paper when they got back home, but the things they chatted about afterwards that would create a sense among lots of people in Britain that they were part of Europe."

"I'd like to think he was right, even though I'm not sure if he actually was. So many people seem to make up their minds on the basis of prejudice that probably goes back to their childhood. Did Mr Chatwell have any countries that you might call 'favourites', or maybe were easier to work with?"

"He often complained about problems with the French. Either there weren't enough British local journalists capable of writing a piece in French or there weren't French journalists who were willing to, or interested in, writing in English. It was different with countries like Portugal or the Czech Republic. They didn't expect anyone to write in their language, and they had young journalists who were competent in English and dead keen to spend a month in the UK. There was no difficulty either in finding willing exchangers in the German regions, but Italy and Spain seemed to be a bit trickier. I expect you'll see that reflected in the files of annual reports."

"You mentioned a Council member being interested in television," I said. "Did the Council members have much influence on policy, or on the choice of places to look for partners? I haven't had time yet to read the minutes."

"Well, of course I don't know what happened in the early years, when the project was starting up," she replied, "but in my time the procedures were well established. Winston always followed up on any suggestions that members made, and sometimes they had useful contacts. But I think the main rôle of Council was to provide a check that everything was being done correctly and to the satisfaction of the Charity Commission. JEEP's aim was educational, not political."

"Yes, I understand that," I replied. "I haven't looked through the names of the members yet, but is there any one of them you think it might be useful to have a talk with?"

She smiled. "I don't know how many of them are still alive. When I was there two former members of Council died; but there were a few younger ones. I remember there was one that Winston used to meet with quite often, and provided him with some really good contacts. He was a crossbencher peer, in the days when all the hereditary peers still sat in the House of Lords. I think he's still alive because I haven't seen an obituary. His name was Viscount Newingham. I remember Winston once said he really understood the philosophy behind JEEP, and not all of the others did."

"I'll look him up," I said, "and hope that he's still hale and hearty. If he's not I'll come back to you for another suggestion. And anyhow I hope we can meet again when I'm getting to the end of my research. If there should be things I'm not certain about I'm sure you'll be able to put me straight."

"I'd be happy to do that," she said, "especially if there's another good lunch involved."

During the rest of lunch Barbara recalled a few incidents which I thought might be useful as light relief in what I expected was likely to be a pretty unexciting narrative.

In the afternoon I returned home to start reading through the annual reports and making notes on the possible structure of the book. I couldn't see any justification for deviating significantly from a chronological pattern. It was, after all, going to be a history, however limited its scope might be.

Biscuits and cheese were enough to satisfy me in the evening; and I relaxed by watching one Cambridge college beat another in 'University Challenge' – and marvelled at the erudition of both.

4

I had to do some picture research for the magazine next morning and it wasn't until after lunchtime baked beans on toast that I returned to research on the book. It was time, I decided, to make draft outlines for the first couple of chapters. How JEEP was actually set up might well be the most interesting part of the story; and I wanted to start writing as soon as possible. By that time in my career I had learned that research for a project can be seductive. One interesting discovery raises the possibility of another that might be even more interesting; but until the actual writing begins the relative importance of all the accumulated facts is difficult to apportion. Some of them contribute to the plot of the story that is being told – there is always a story – and some are purely ornamental.

So I decided to have a quick look at my one unexplored source of information before I started putting pen to paper (an expression that was literally accurate because, since I did my first published writing by hand in the absence of any kind of keyboard, when I was on a holiday in Aruba, I have always preferred to write my first drafts in long hand). I picked up the box full of Winston Chatwell's diaries that I had acquired in Hove and opened it.

As Chatwell's nephew had warned me, the first of the black-covered A6 notebooks that I looked into was written in a terse, telegraphic style. The first date was Monday, September 5, 1983, and the entry read:

Starting new job, so it may be worth keeping some kind of personal record. Inspected office suite on floor above the Bodley European Educational Trust in Buckingham Palace Road. Old-fashioned layout but should be comfortable for projected staff of five or six. Made list of furniture needed. BEET Finance Officer, John Jones, gave some helpful suggestions. Afternoon meeting of JEEP Management Council. Four members including Bodley in chair, but he intends to appoint two more when suitable people available. Most of time spent on finalizing statement of objectives and arrangements for registering with Charity Commission. BEET solicitor will help with that. Agreed that I should go ahead with advertising for finance officer, logistics officer and most urgently, a PA. Think FO and LO can share a secretarial assistant, who could also be telephonist.

Evening to 'Pit' at Barbican, to see Bulgakov's 'Molière'. A bit convoluted but David Troughton very good.

I flipped through some more entries, which were even terser, and speculated that the diaries were unlikely to add much to what I could learn from the official files. However, about a fortnight further into the diary job interviews had begun and Chatwell's brief comments on the interviewees made for more interesting reading. In those politically incorrect days the procedures seemed to be incredibly informal, and I concluded that each final choice was the person he felt he would be most comfortable working with.

The first choice he made, from among four candidates, was of a Personal Assistant. She was named Sumintra Chopra, and was described as "of Indian ethnicity, from a family who fled the ghastly regime in Guyana that ruined the country after it became independent. Can start work on 1st October." I cross-checked in the Personnel File and saw that Miss Chopra had a degree in Geography and French from University College, London and had recently completed a three-month secretarial course.

His next appointment was a Logistics Officer, and in the three interviews for the post he had the help of the BEET Finance Officer, John Jones. They chose a man who had been a warrant officer in the Army's Logistic Corps before retiring when he got married and started a family. His name was Basil Singleton. On the same day he also appointed a Secretarial Assistant, a young woman who had been getting 'work experience' in BEET after completing a secretarial course. She was called Olivia Heyman.

Finding a Finance Officer proved to be more difficult. With the assistance of Jones he had interviewed four candidates without success by the end of September, at which point I took a break from reading the diary. I needed to begin some research on the Internet for my next *Great Captains* article, which was going to be on William Marshal, Earl of Pembroke.

On the following day I returned to leafing through the diary, and saw that a Finance Officer was eventually appointed on October 8. She was Helen Braithwaite, described as "mother of two teenagers, wanting change from working in Unilever – from small fish in big pond to big fish in small pond."

In subsequent entries Chatwell listed newspapers and periodicals, both in Britain and on the Continent, to which he sent introductory information about the Exchange Programme. The countries included Italy, Spain and Portugal. It was on October 22 that he made the first mention of introductory letters being sent to editors in the UK.

References in the diary to activities or events outside work were few and cryptic. I noted that he seemed to approve of the success of Neil Kinnock and Roy Hattersley at the Brighton Labour Party Conference at the beginning of October; and at the end of the month he enjoyed a play at the Barbican Theatre called "Maydays". He described it as "a discerning look at the disillusionment of left-wing idealism over 30 years."

The second entry in November was longer than average, and I sensed that it might be important. It began with a satisfied comment on the arrival in the post of four interested responses from editors on the Continent. This was followed by an unexpected visit from Herbert Bodley. The diary entry said:

Mr Bodley apologized for looking in without warning, but said something had come up unexpectedly. His sister had been in touch with him about her daughter, who is looking for a job –

name is Perdita Preston. She graduated at Cambridge this year in Italian, French and something else (think he said Philosophy). Got an Upper Second, but according to her mother it would have been a First if she'd spent more time on study and less on social life. Apparently she'd had plans for a marriage but these had collapsed dramatically, and she'd gone travelling in Europe. Now she was back and wanted to immerse herself in work, but not in teaching, which she thought would be too demanding in her present state of mind.

Mr Bodley's suggestion was she might join us as a translator and research assistant. He said if I was agreeable he would ask her to come for an interview with me; but if I didn't think she would fit in I must say so and that would be the end of the matter. I mustn't feel under any pressure. But she was a very pleasant girl, and highly intelligent, and he hoped she might be an asset in helping to get JEEP 'off the ground'.

Naturally I agreed to see her; and he thought she would be available for an interview on Monday. She is living with her parents in Cheam and so should have no problem with travel.

Since the next diary entry was for a Saturday it was characteristically terse. He did some shopping in Waitrose, and he had his hair cut. In the evening he went to the Curzon Cinema to see a film called "Betrayal", starring Ben Kingsley and Jeremy Irons, and rated it "very good". The Sunday entry was equally brief. He went to an exhibition about Prince Albert at the Royal College of Arts; and in the evening he read several newspapers, making only one comment: "Interesting article in Sunday Times on 'A life in the day of Moira Stuart'."

The interview with Perdita Preston duly took place on the Monday, and he recorded it in some detail:

Saw Perdita Preston, as arranged. Attractive looking girl, but she had 'dressed down' in grey sweater and jeans. Seemed almost shy at first, but think that when she realized I was well disposed towards her she relaxed and talked freely. No doubt about her intelligence, and once she understood what we are aiming to do she seemed genuinely enthusiastic. Decided she would fit in very well and asked her when she could start. To my surprise, she said she'd like to start work tomorrow, and I agreed, and said it would be simplest to calculate her salary as beginning from today – which seemed to please her. Will get her to start preparing an annotated list of Italian periodicals tomorrow.

On the following day he simply recorded that "Perdita Preston started work. Seemed to grasp immediately what was required." He also had a conversation with someone at the London Magazine Branch of the NUJ about the possibility of addressing a meeting of the Branch.

I put down the diary feeling that I was now ready to begin writing the narrative.

5

Next morning I began writing the first chapter. I had no need to exercise my brain on devising an arresting opening paragraph, because it was unlikely that anyone without a prior interest in the Journalists' European Exchange Programme would ever look inside the book. For about an hour I progressed quite rapidly with the writing, explaining the context within which Herbert Bodley had decided to establish the project in 1983. The temptation to take a break for coffee was just beginning to intrude when the telephone rang.

The caller was Tom Gibbs an old friend from my student days whom I hadn't seen for over a year. In my final year at Bristol I had shared a flat with him and two other fellow-students; and I had continued to see quite a lot of him in the following year, when he was doing a Master's at Imperial College and I was doing one at the LSE. However, after that our paths had gone in different directions and, although we had kept in touch, we had been able to meet only about once a year. So I was pleased to know that he was in town, and arranged to have lunch with him in the Caffé Piccolo.

When we had settled at the table and given our orders to Giovanni Tom asked, "So what are you up to these days? Have you sold many copies of that biography?"

"A couple of thousand, the publishers tell me. It's about what they had hoped for. I'm just starting now on another book. It's the history of a trust-funded organization that operated from 1983 to 2008. It was called the Journalists' European Exchange Project, or JEEP for short. Doing the history at this particular moment is a little bit poignant don't you think? The aim of the project was to help people understand things that Britain had in common with European countries, and vice versa – at the local community level. It was designed for journalists working in local or regional media. I suppose Brexit's going to have an impact on your line of work, like everything else."

"Microelectronics certainly won't be exempt, but it's hard to predict what the effect will be," he replied. "I suppose a lot will depend on whether or not it's a No Deal Brexit. The bosses are worried, I know; and we've just cancelled plans for recruiting three new staff. I was going to be on an interviewing panel. I was hoping the job might attract somebody with beauty as well as brains."

"Does that mean you haven't got anything going for you at the moment?" I asked.

"I just don't seem to have the right social contacts," he said, "and I'm certainly not going to waste my time on Tinder. The Internet is strictly for work as far as I'm concerned. But I'm usually too flaked out in the evenings to go to the kind of places where you can meet interesting women.

"I know the place where I work is a big organization with quite a few intelligent women around, but getting started is a problem these days, isn't it? All this 'Me Too' business makes you a bit wary. Last year we had a memo circulated saying that care should be taken not to invade the personal space of colleagues – although I haven't yet heard about anybody being given a hard time. Now that I seem to be getting work more under control I think I'll start looking around again. What about you? Last Christmas you mentioned going out with an Italian girl."

"Unfortunately that didn't come to anything," I replied. "Gina went home to Milan before… we really got it together. But last week I started getting to know somebody who might just be a possibility. She's a solicitor. I've been working with her for a while, and she did me a good turn – without me asking. She recommended me for the book commission."

"Sounds promising," said Tom. "But if she's a solicitor you'll need to be careful. She might slap an injunction on you before you know what's happening."

We both laughed; and at that moment Giovanni brought us our first course.

That evening, having noted that there was nothing on television I had the least desire to watch, I decided to scan some more of Chatwell's diary in preparation for writing the second chapter. I hoped I might find some 'human interest' to enliven the account of how JEEP began its work.

Resuming the scan in November 1983, I found that the entries were mainly brief and almost telegraphic. Chatwell seemed to be occupied with innumerable interviews and telephone conversations with trustees and the contacts that they gave him – some of whom had names that I recognized. But he recorded very little about the content of those conversations, confining himself to comments such as 'helpful', 'useful', or 'waste of time'.

On November 12 he noted that Perdita Preston had started work, but didn't refer to her again until November 16, when he observed, "Perdita appears to be settling in well." On the same day he noted that "Sumintra was very helpful with travel arrangements for next week." In the week that followed he travelled, by train, to meet editors in Glasgow, Selkirk, Durham and Derby – describing all his contacts as 'useful' or 'helpful' or 'productive'.

In spite of his strenuous itinerary he was back in the office on Friday, and the diary entry for that day was longer than usual. It began by noting favourable replies that had been received from editors in the Netherlands and Portugal, and continued:

> *Invited Perdita to have lunch with me at the Capri, to tell her about meetings with editors – and also to find out a little more about her, if she wanted to open up. She did, a lot more than I had expected. Began by asking about her recent experience of university in Perugia. Seems to have found it easy academically, and said the social life had been "even more hectic" than Cambridge. Then she added, "but in the end it didn't work out very well. I don't want to talk about it."*

26

No doubt that was the unhappy relationship her uncle had alluded to. I asked her whether she had visited Venice and she replied enthusiastically. Said she'd only had a day there and wanted to go back for a longer stay. Confessed that she and a fellow-student (female) who accompanied her to Venice had stolen the tip left on an outside table at a café and used it to buy coffee, because they'd spent all their cash.

She also said she wanted to rent a flat in London, to save time travelling and also to make it easier to go to the theatre and concerts. I said that seemed a good idea if she could find a place at a reasonable rent. She hesitated and then said, very quickly, "I also want to get away from home. My parents are constantly squabbling. Being away at university I hadn't realized how far they'd grown apart – though I don't think they're going to separate." Or words to that effect.

Surprised at how frank she'd been. I made sympathetic noises, and then said if she needed to take time off to look at possible flats that could easily be arranged. Seemed to be grateful.

Conversation could easily have gone on much longer, but I'd agreed to see Mrs Braithwaite at 2.30. Useful discussion about petty cash, etc.

I was intrigued by the uncharacteristic amount of detail that Chatwell had included in this entry, and wondered if he might have begun to develop a special interest in Perdita. It was irrelevant to my own narrative but it might give me a clearer picture of the kind of person he was.

Diary entries for the following week were once again brief and cryptic. They referred mainly to meetings with members of staff and plans to have some re-decoration work on the premises.

Plans were finalized for the first exchange visit to be made in January, by a Belgian journalist to a newspaper in Suffolk, and Chatwell wrote to him with a suggestion about a story that he might follow up, concerning Belgian refugees during the First World War.

On December 2 Perdita had asked Chatwell for time off on the following Monday to view a flat, and this led to another long diary entry:

Perdita asked, very hesitantly, if I might possibly have time to look at the flat with her. She didn't want to ask her mother, because her mother wasn't really in favour of her leaving home; and she'd never had any experience of looking at property before. Said I would if she could arrange viewing in the lunchtime period, which she was able to do.

The flat was in a purpose-built block of about a dozen, in a side street off The Cut, quite close to Waterloo Station. We were shown round by an eager young man from the estate agents, who at first thought I was Perdita's father, and was embarrassed when told that I wasn't. The flat was compact, with bedroom, bathroom, kitchen and small reception room, and was well maintained, with basic, but quite pleasant furnishings. Advised her that she was unlikely to find anything better at such a reasonable rental, and so she decided to take a one-year lease.

On the way back to the office she was very animated and chatted about a flat she'd shared in her final year at Cambridge, on the road to Grantchester. We swapped lines from 'The Old Vicarage'. As I parted from her in her office she suddenly kissed me on the cheek, and then said, "Maybe I shouldn't have done that, but I'm so grateful for your help."

Laughed and said, "It's the nicest thing anyone has done to me for a very long time." Noticed that when she smiles her face is really beautiful.

With Basil and Sumintra went through final details for the painting to be done in week after Christmas. Will extend staff holiday by two days. Basil not going to be away and said he would keep an eye on the work.

As I closed the diary and began to prepare for bed I reflected that it might turn out to be more interesting than I had expected; but it was also unlikely to add anything significant to the material I need to round out the book I was writing, and so I must be careful not to spend too much time on it.

6

Over the next week I spent a good deal of time on completing my article about Robert Blake and also on researching some illustrations for the next issue at the editor's request. And I managed as well to make a start on the second chapter of the book. My next consultation with Judith would not be for a fortnight and I had a strong desire to see her again much sooner. I wanted to find out if she was in a relationship with anyone else – there was no ring on the significant finger – because if she was I would stop wasting time thinking about her. The lunch we'd had could be construed as just a token of gratitude, but if I were to invite her out now, before our next professional encounter, it would be a clear signal that I wanted to get to know her. It would also give her an opportunity to indicate that she wasn't interested.

There was nothing I could do about it at the weekend because I didn't have a private phone number for her. On Monday morning, however, I resolved to test the water. I thought it best to wait until late morning, when she might have finished dealing with anything urgent that had come to her desk over the weekend. As she didn't have a direct line I had to speak first to the formidable Miss Hardcastle, but fortunately she recognized my name and put me through without enquiring my business. Judith sounded genuinely pleased to hear from me, and I asked whether she had yet seen the new exhibition at the National Gallery, featuring the Spanish Impressionist painter, Sorolla.

"No. I've read a review that said it's very good. Have you seen it?" she replied.

"I haven't, and I was planning to go on Saturday. I wondered if you might like to come with me. I always think it's more interesting if you're able to discuss what you see with someone else – someone who shares your interest, of course. If you are interested I thought maybe you might like to have lunch with me, either before or after looking at the exhibition.

I think I actually held my breath while I waited for her reply. If she said yes it could be the beginning of another voyage of exploration. My previous adventures with women, although providing some moments of pleasure, had all ended in frustration.

She said. "That's a great idea. It's always nice to have someone to discuss with, even if they disagree with you. Could we have lunch afterwards? I'll need to do some food shopping in the morning before I meet you. This week it's my turn to go to John Barnes, with Georgina. I could be at the National Gallery by about half-eleven. Would that be all right?"

I was delighted, and surprised that my invitation had been accepted so readily. Maybe she'd been waiting for me to follow-up on our first encounter. Quickly I agreed the details of time and place, and resisted the temptation to say more, being aware that I was ringing her in work time and others might overhear. If all went well I hoped soon to be in possession of her personal telephone number.

Although it would be a week before I actually saw Judith again I now had a feeling of contentment that enabled me to settle down to the not very exciting task of writing another chapter of the history of JEEP. I had moved to the point where there were some cuttings to be consulted of the first articles resulting from the Programme, and that task absorbed me until the late afternoon. In the hope that his diary might reveal some personal reaction to these first tokens of success I then turned again to the volume in which I had marked with a Daunt's bookmark the end of my previous scan.

On December 9 Chatwell had a discussion with all the members of staff about arrangements for the Christmas holiday, and it was decided that the office would be closed from December 24 to January 3. He noted that "Perdita remarked she didn't want to have to spend any more time at home with the family." In the following week he decided to buy Christmas presents for Perdita and Sumintra. In Marks and Spencer at Marble Arch he bought an amaryllis ('Apple Blossom' variety) for each of them. The presents were handed over on the day before Christmas Eve, and both recipients expressed delight. He recorded that Perdita said,

"It's just what I need to brighten up the flat." Sumintra was going to keep hers in her office.

Entries over the Christmas holiday period were brief. He spent four days with his parents, who were living in Broadstairs, and recorded that on Boxing Day his sister, Margaret, and her family came to visit. His nephew, Gordon, who gave me the diaries, wasn't mentioned by name, but simply referred to as "her teenage son and daughter." He returned to London for a day and then took off for a six-day holiday in Rome.

The Rome entries were a little more detailed and recorded visits to several churches, each with its 'Christmas Crib' elaborately portrayed in idiosyncratic surroundings. He commented: "It looks as if the churches are competing with one another to have the most improbable Nativity tableau." The Vatican museums got a couple of sentences.

He was back at work on January 3, and noted that Perdita told him she had moved into her new flat, with help from her brother, who was home on vacation from university. This had prompted him to write at the end of the day's entry, "Must get a flat-warming present for her."

It was not until four days later, on Saturday, that he found time to go shopping for the present, at John Lewis in Oxford Street. He selected a "large wooden fruit bowl costing £5, and when I took to the counter to pay was given a $12_{1/2}$ per cent discount in the January sale."

On the Sunday evening he watched the first episode of a new television drama called *The Thorn Birds* and described it as "pure soap opera but compulsively watchable." So it was on Monday morning, in the privacy of her office, that he presented Perdita with her flat-warming present. He recorded that:

> *She seemed very delighted and kissed me warmly on both cheeks. Possibly because I'd said I hoped she wouldn't think it presumptuous of me to give her a present, she then said, "Oh, I love getting presents. Now I must decide where's the best place to put it. Maybe you'd like to come round*

one day and see how I've fixed things." Said I'd like that.

I was particularly interested in the next day's entry, when Chatwell had a meeting with someone from Unilever, to explore possibilities that might arise because the firm had activities located in both Britain and the Netherlands. My interest arose from the fact that it was in 1984 that my father went to work at Unilever, and there met my mother, who had already been working at its headquarters for a couple of years as a secretary. Of course I didn't expect to find any reference to one of them. That would have been too much of a coincidence. But it seemed that the meeting was productive, and so there might well be future references to things that happened at the company. In the Friday entry of that week Chatwell wrote:

> *Asked Perdita if she would be interested in coming with me to a Festival Hall concert on Sunday afternoon – Handel and Mozart. She seemed genuinely pleased and said yes. Asked, a bit tentatively, if she'd like to have a meal beforehand but she said she was going to have a lot of weekend chores to do. Booked tickets on way home.*

On the Sunday he wrote:

> *Concert went well and Perdita seemed really to enjoy it. James Galway playing two Mozart flute concertos was particularly good. Not much opportunity for conversation except in interval. Seems to have settled into her flat with help from her brother, who stayed there for a couple of nights. Gathered that he, too, is unhappy about their parents' constant squabbling. Gave me a kiss on the cheek when we parted.*

There was a lunch meeting on the following Tuesday with a journalist from Essex who was planning an exchange visit to Belgium, and Chatwell invited Perdita to take part. He noted afterwards:

> *Williamson seemed to become more interested in chatting-up Perdita than in discussing the purpose of the exchange. Afraid this time she was a bit of a distraction. Understandable, since he must have been in his twenties. Maybe I should reserve using her reinforcement for negotiations with crusty old editors or female executives.*

However, in the following week he took her with him to a Brussels-sponsored media conference, and noted with approval that she had talked in the lunch interval to the deputy editor of a Sunday newspaper, although, since national newspapers were not included in JEEP, that was not going to be directly useful. He recorded the conference as "a waste of time."

The deputy editor, whose name was Tom Wells, was mentioned again three days later, when Perdita informed Chatwell that he had invited her to have lunch with him at the RAC on the following Monday. That day's diary entry also contained a short reference to an article which had appeared in a Rotterdam newspaper, for which they were going to need a translator.

On the Monday Chatwell wrote:

> *When Perdita returned from her lunch with Wells she came to see me and seemed to be pleased with what had happened. They had talked mainly about Cambridge. Wells was at Trinity about fifteen years ago. He was very keen to meet her again and said he would take her to Ronnie Scott's one evening, and would give her a call when he could find a free date. When I asked if*

she liked him she said he was "all right." Then, when she was just about to leave, she said she'd been with Williamson on Saturday night. She added, "I don't think I'll see him again. He's too possessive" When I asked, "In what way?" she replied, "He reminded me of an Australian guy I spent a night with in a youth hostel in Greece. Next morning he was acting as if he owned me. So I just cut him dead, and he couldn't understand what had happened." She gave a little chuckle and turned to leave. My guess is that she'd spent the night with Williamson.

The diary was beginning to be more interesting than I had expected; but my stomach was telling me that I needed some food, and so I re-inserted the bookmark at January 31.

7

I met Judith, as arranged, at the entrance to the Sainsbury Wing of the National Gallery. Her professional work image had been discarded and her dark brown hair cascaded freely down her back to about six inches below her neck. She was wearing light blue jeans and a burgundy-coloured sweater with a high neck, under a short black padded raincoat. Had she not still been wearing the same glasses I might not have recognized her. Although she seemed genuinely pleased to see me I thought it would be premature to engage her in 'air kissing'.

We both enjoyed the "Sorolla: Spanish Master of Light" exhibition. In one room Judith exclaimed, "He really did know how to capture the sunshine. I felt warm just looking at that picture." And I responded, "It's strange how such a talented painter could be forgotten for decades. I thought I must have read at some time or another about all the leading Impressionists and yet I can't ever remember seeing his name. I suppose his reputation got overshadowed by the arrival of people like Picasso and Miro and Salvador Dali."

At my suggestion we took the Tube from Charing Cross and went to the Caffé Piccolo for lunch. On Saturday the diners were different from a weekday – mainly tourists. When he saw Judith Giovanni gave me a knowing look; and he was very attentive during lunch.

While we were waiting for the first course Judith asked me, "How are you getting on with the book?"

I replied that the writing was going ahead quite well, and added, "My research is uncovering some unexpected information about Chatwell, the Director of JEEP. He may have been a more complex character than appeared at first sight."

"Does that mean you might actually have a sub-plot about mysterious goings-on behind the scenes?" she asked.

"I'm afraid that's not very likely. It's just that he's been observing the unusual behaviour of a female member of staff, and it's pretty clear that he likes her. She's very attractive, and she also seems to be promiscuous; so I'd be surprised if anything developed between them. And even if it did I would be surprised if it had any bearing on what I'm supposed to be writing. I'm just interested to see how the relationship develops."

"Who's going to be the subject of your next magazine article?" Judith asked, just as our ravioli arrived at the table.

"It's going to be Sir John Moore. Have you heard of him?"

She smiled, and began to recite:

> *We buried him darkly at dead of night,*
> *The sods with our bayonets turning.*

And I joined in at the next line:

> *By the struggling moonbeam's misty light*
> *And the lanthorn dimly burning.*

"I'm surprised that you had to learn that particular poem," I said.

"We had an English Literature teacher, Miss Pearson, when I was in the Second Form who was very enthusiastic about Nineteenth Century Romantic poetry, and she was also very insistent on the importance of learning a lot of poems by heart. I think I agree with her about that. But does Sir John Moore really qualify as a 'Great Captain'? Not that I know very much about him, I'm afraid."

"Obviously I think he does," I replied. "He deserves a lot of credit for getting the British Army into the state where it was capable of defeating Napoleon, even though he didn't live to lead it in the decisive battles. And, of course, Corunna was a kind of early version of Dunkirk, and so it gives the war gamers among the readership something to intrigue them. That's quite important because the latest survey for the magazine found that about a third of the readers are war game enthusiasts."

"Was military history a particular interest of yours before you got the commission to write for *Great Captains*?" Judith asked.

"Actually it wasn't. Like a lot of important things that happen in life, getting the work was really an accident. I'd been hoping to get into some kind of political journalism, without much success. When I was visiting my parents in Delft I met one of the PR people in Shell, and when I mentioned that I was looking for work in journalism he told me about a magazine group in London he had been visiting because they ran an oil industry journal. He'd had lunch with the editor, who mentioned that the group was launching a popular history magazine, and actually asked him if he knew of anyone who might be interested in joining their team of freelance writers. This had happened only about two days earlier and so I followed up the lead straight away. Personal contacts can be so important. Have you had any experiences like that?"

"Oh, yes," she said. "I'd originally wanted to study Art History and then I met an old schoolfriend of my mother's, who was a solicitor in the City, and she told me what an exciting job it was, with lots of interesting clients that she met every day. And she was also making a lot of money. So I decided I'd do Law, and make Art my hobby. And by good luck just before I graduated she heard about the vacancy and tipped me off; and I was lucky enough to get the job when I applied. I think it helped that I was a woman and the firm was wanting to 'diversify'. You can never really tell what tips the balance, can you?"

"That's true. In my case I think I was the only applicant."

"Have you decided who you're going to write about after you've buried Sir John Moore?" she asked.

"I think it's going to be Gustavus Adolphus. There's no question about him being called 'great' – the Swedish parliament actually made it official. And there will be plenty of battle plans for the war gamers to play with."

"I don't think I've ever seen a painting of him, although I'm sure there must be some," she said.

"I'm going to have to do some research on that. I expect that being in the far north, apart from when he was invading Germany, he didn't have contact with any of the great artists of that time. He would have been a very suitable subject for Rubens, wouldn't he?"

"Yes. He doesn't sound like the kind of person who would have sat for Rembrandt. You said you've been to Holland a lot; so I suppose you've seen all the Rembrandts over there."

"I probably have," I replied. "There are a lot of very good galleries in different parts of the country. But for a comprehensive collection of art from all over Europe I think our National Gallery is hard to beat."

"I agree," she said, "though I probably haven't seen as many others as you have."

The possibility that she might become a travelling companion flashed through my mind as I responded. "Apart from in the Netherlands I haven't really seen very many. It's something I'm looking forward to – visiting new art galleries. But I'll need to earn some more money to fund the travelling."

"I know," she said. "It's lucky there are so many bargains to be had nowadays. I'm afraid I'm not conscience-stricken about saving the planet by staying on the ground. That plane's going to take off anyhow, regardless of whether or not I'm in the bargain seat."

"I feel the same," I said. "I'm all in favour of more research to speed up the time when planes will be electric-powered, and I read somewhere last week that the first experimental one is about to be tested."

Wary about getting further into political topics at this stage in our relationship, I asked, "Do you like classical music? I went to a wonderful concert at the Festival Hall last Sunday, with the Philharmonia."

"Really?" she exclaimed. "I was there with my flat-mate, Georgina. She's keener on music than I am, but I sometimes go to concerts with her. I really enjoyed the Mozart piano concerto. Do you play anything yourself?"

"Afraid not. I only started being interested in music when I came back to London after Bristol, and there was the chance then to listen to really great performers." I omitted to say that I had started going to concerts in order to enjoy the company of a girlfriend, but that relationship had lasted for only three months. "Do you ever go to the Wigmore Hall?"

"I've been a couple of times. I don't much care for the lay-out, but they do have some great performers."

"Because, being a freelance, I'm able to control my own time, I've been to a few of their lunchtime concerts," I said. "It's within walking distance of your office, but I suppose it would mean you'd have to take around a half-hour extra at your lunch hour – and not have any lunch."

"I might be able to manage one, if it wasn't on a busy day," she said. "My boss is well aware that in most weeks I actually work more hours than I'm paid for, and he's relaxed about lunch hours. Having said that, however, just at the moment I'm keen to demonstrate how dedicated I am to the job. There's shortly going to be a vacancy for an associate, and I'm hoping I'll get the promotion."

"I can see that visibility could be quite important," I said. "I'm afraid the work you do for the magazine doesn't provide much opportunity to pull off a spectacular coup. Maybe I should get the editor to write in and tell them that you've saved us from a catastrophic copyright claim."

She laughed, and her eyes sparkled in a way that I'd noticed several times when we were talking about favourite pictures in the gallery. "That's a nice idea," she said, "but I think I'll just have to keep adding to my Brownie points on the boring jobs. It reminds me of a lecturer we had at university who tried to get approving comments from his students in one of those surveys that they've started doing. At the time we didn't know he was in the running for a professorship."

She then told me a mildly amusing story about academic politicking. It really interested me because of what it revealed about her easy relationship with friends, and her sense of fun. I remembered an amusing episode in students' union politics that happened when I was doing my master's degree at the LSE, and she laughed when I told her about it, her eyes lighting up again with that sparkle.

When we'd finished our main course I persuaded her to try Giovanni's tiramisu. She made a remark about still trying to compensate for having put on weight through over-indulgence at Christmas and I asked, "Do you really need to be trying to improve on perfection?"

She blushed slightly and the sparkle was back in her eyes as she surprised me by saying, "Flattery will get you everywhere."

Relieved that my attempt at a compliment had not been rebuffed, I said, "Giovanni will be happy that you're ready to sample his desserts. Maybe we could do this again after I bring you our copyright problems on Wednesday week?"

To my delight she replied, "Oh, yes. I'd like to do that." However, my mounting hope that we might be able to extend our time together that afternoon was quashed when she went on to say, "I'm afraid I'm going to have to leave fairly soon because I've promised to meet Henrietta at John Lewis. She's choosing a coat to wear at a wedding in May and wants my moral support."

But my hopes remained high when we parted outside the restaurant and I dared to go through the motions of an air kiss on both cheeks. Her lips pouted briefly in response, and I resolved that next time I would be bold enough to make physical contact.

8

On the following Monday morning I returned to writing the JEEP history, after I had finished reading an account of how Roger Federer had won his hundred-and-first championship, in Miami, on the previous day. The chapter was concerned mainly with quoting articles that had resulted from the first round of European contacts made by Chatwell. Some were predictable but others displayed considerable originality on the part of the, mainly, young, (I suspected) journalists involved. By lunchtime I had finished the chapter, and I listened to 'The World at One' while I ate my cheese on toast. Rumour had it that Theresa May might be going to strike a deal with the Opposition on the Brexit negotiations.

Feeling satisfied with the progress I'd made on the book, I decided to indulge myself with another browse through Chatwell's diaries. I picked up the story in February 1984, when he was starting to receive copies of articles that resulted from some of the first journalistic exchanges. One of them I remembered seeing in the file. It was a long piece from an Italian newspaper which followed up on the story of a British soldier who had escaped from a German prisoner-of-war camp and been assisted by the locals in a village. The man had actually taken a holiday to revisit the village while a journalist from his home town was on an exchange visit on the area. The story had been published in the papers at both ends of the exchange – with an appropriate Italian translation, of course.

Chatwell wrote:

Perdita checked the translation and found that it was pretty faithful to the original. Then she told me that Wells had rung her with an invitation to Ronnie Scott's on Saturday. She had decided to accept, and seemed to be quite excited.

The rest of that week's entries contained nothing of particular interest and I turned to the following Monday wondering if she would confide in Chatwell about what had happened during her Saturday night encounter. I had vague memories of having read one or two mentions in newspapers of the later stages of the noteworthy career of Tom Wells. She did, indeed, report on what had happened. Chatwell wrote:

> *When we had finished checking the diary Perdita told me that Ronnie Scott's had been a bit of a disappointment. Said she wasn't all that keen on that kind of music, and it was also very smoky. Afterwards Wells had invited her to go home with him but she had declined, saying that she was very tired. When she was telling me that she gave a little grin and said, "Sometimes it's good to keep them waiting awhile, just when they think they've scored." I asked if he'd been in touch again and she said he'd rung on Sunday evening, inviting her to have lunch with him at the RAC on Wednesday. She asked if she could take extra time off for the lunch and I assented – on condition (smiling) that she told me about the outcome. She said, "Oh yes. I'll want to talk to you about it."*

Diary entries for the next two days were brief, with the arrival of copies of two letters published in the Italian newspaper and translated by Perdita, as the principal interest. On the Wednesday afternoon Chatwell had a meeting at the NUJ, and so it wasn't until Thursday that Perdita told him about her lunch. He wrote:

> *Perdita said that Wells asked her to have supper at his flat next Sunday, adding it was pretty clear that meant breakfast on Monday morning would be included. She hasn't decided yet whether to accept. Said he was "attractive but a bit intense."*

They had talked about her name, because Wells asked if her parents had been Shakespeare enthusiasts and named her after the heroine of 'The Winter's Tale'. She has replied that her mother had actually played the part of Perdita in a school production, and had wanted to be an actress but her parents opposed the idea and she trained as a secretary.

Perdita then asked about my name, saying she'd never before met anyone called Winston. When I said that I'd been born in 1943 she instantly understood the connection. I wonder if Wells's intentions might be 'honourable'. Have a feeling she would like them to be.

For the remainder of the week nothing else in the diary was of particular interest. I turned to the entry for the following Monday curious to know what had happened in Perdita's encounter with Wells. True to form, she was frank in her report back to Chatwell.

Looked into Perdita's office mid-morning and she said, "I expect you'd like to know what happened with Tom," and I replied, "Only if you want to tell me." Wells's flat (somewhere in Bloomsbury) had been, she said, very much a bachelor pad, with little decoration and just a few modern prints on the walls – but lots of books. The supper had been quite lavish, even including caviar and two very nice wines. He had dropped a lot of names of famous people he said that he knew well. After they'd drunk quite a lot of wine he'd suggested they go into the bedroom and she'd agreed.

"He was all right," she said, "but maybe not as good as he thought he was." Then she said that at breakfast Wells had told her a secret – which I mustn't repeat to anyone else. He had been

approached by a new television channel in Canada with an offer to become their head of news and current affairs. She went on to say that he'd asked her if she'd ever thought about living in Canada. When she'd replied that she hadn't he had said, "Maybe you ought to" – with an enigmatic smile.

"Was that all?" I asked her, and she replied that it was; but he'd asked her to go for supper and spend the night again on Wednesday. I said, "Don't be late for work on Thursday morning," and we both laughed. Looks as if he's contemplating an offer of marriage. He couldn't expect her to go to Canada on any other terms. Her job wouldn't be difficult to fill but I'd still miss her if she went.

I was curious to find out what the Thursday entry would reveal, and I think Chatwell had been curious too. He wrote:

Went to Perdita's office after I'd been through correspondence with Sumintra. She seemed eager to tell me that Wells had again talked about Canada, but had also got into a lengthy discussion about marriage, starting by telling her that his first marriage had gone wrong because he and his wife hadn't got to know each other properly before they got married. Perdita thought it was about five years ago that he got divorced. He had then implied that he wanted her to get to know him properly before they talked about marriage. I said something like "Nothing wrong with that" and she agreed, saying, "I think he was being sincere." He had asked her to go to his flat again on Sunday evening and she had agreed.

The only item of interest on Friday was a note about a newspaper in Normandy which had been in touch and was anxious to take part in an exchange. I had already written in the book about the early success which had resulted from that contact, memories of D-Day having provided a focus for the articles. On Saturday Chatwell wrote about visiting the Wallace Collection to see a recently restored Titian, 'Perseus and Andromeda.'.

On the Monday Perdita once again reported back on her encounter with Wells. He had been very "enthusiastic" she said; and he had talked about his need to avoid being gossiped about, which was something he hadn't mentioned before. Chatwell wrote:

> *I asked her if anything more had been said about Canada, and she replied that it hadn't. She thought he was waiting to hear about the final outcome of the job negotiations. But she did seem to be thinking seriously about the possibility of moving to Canada – and the prospect of marriage. If it happens I will be sorry to see her go.*

I was about to turn to the next page of the diary when the telephone rang. It was the Editor, wanting me to find an additional illustration for an article on Fabius Maximus Cunctator, due to appear in the 'Ancient History' section of the next edition. The author had been able to come up with only one. I couldn't resist the temptation to say, "OK, I'll get on to the search without delay," but I think the irony may have been lost on the Editor, who might not yet have read the article.

However, I did reluctantly put aside Chatwell's diary and begin my picture search.

9

It was not until the following day that I found a suitable illustration for the article on Fabius Cunctator. In the end I had to resort to using a picture of his more famous adversary, Hannibal. Determined to eschew employing a hackneyed image of elephants crossing the Alps, I discovered a painting by an obscure Victorian artist which portrayed the frustrated Carthaginian gazing at the distant walls of Rome. I would need to check the copyright situation at my next meeting with Judith.

For a couple of hours I then worked on the next chapter of the JEEP history. It consisted mainly of articles which had appeared in Italian newspapers and had been, I presume, translated by Perdita. At lunchtime I made myself a cheese sandwich and, remembering to pocket the key to the gate, took it into the Dorset Square garden to have lunch. There was a brief period of sunshine and I sat admiring the cherry blossom as I ate; but the air was still chilly and I didn't linger for very long.

Having used only about half of my self-imposed lunch hour I decided to indulge in another short browse in Winston Chatwell's diary. I was curious to discover whether Perdita's latest admirer, the journalist whose name was vaguely familiar to me, had actually proposed to her. In the next entry which mentioned her name Chatwell wrote:

> *Perdita said there had been no further mention of Canada (and, I presume, no marriage proposal). However, she does seem to be getting used to the idea. Saw copy of a guidebook to Canada on her desk. I think she was deliberately changing the subject when she started telling me about how she once had a holiday job in Foyle's. She didn't really enjoy it – 'in spite of being surrounded by books'.*

I turned over the page of the diary and saw that the next day's entry ran to a second page. It began with a short account of a meeting with a journalist from Cardiff who was interested in going to Portugal. He then noted that Perdita had asked to extend her lunch hour so that she could visit a hairdresser in Victoria Street. Next he wrote:

Much sooner than I had expected her, Perdita came into my office looking distressed, and it was evident that her hair had not been altered. She sat down by my desk and I asked what was the matter. While waiting to have her hair done she'd picked up a magazine – she thought it was 'The Tatler' – and in it she'd seen a photo of Tom Wells with his arm around a glamorous-looking woman in a low-cut dress. The caption described him as a leading Fleet Street journalist, and said she was heiress to a Canadian 'media magnate' who died last year, leaving her joint owner, with her brother, of a company that controlled several television and radio stations. Her name was either Mackintosh or Macintyre – Perdita couldn't remember which. I asked if it was a recent edition of the magazine or just one that had been lying around for a long time, and she said she'd checked the date and it was last week. The caption also said that Wells had been seen 'spending a lot of time' in her company in recent weeks.'

I said that Wells might just have been cultivating the lady's company for business reasons, but Perdita thought it didn't look like that in the photograph. She was sure that the reason why he had been a bit secretive about exactly what was happening with the Canadian job was somehow connected with this woman. When I suggested that she might confront him she rejected that idea because she didn't want to appear 'untrustful' if there really was no reason to doubt him. It might undermine their relationship if he thought she was the jealous type. I hoped that before very long Wells would speak to her about it without needing to be prompted.

Keen to discover what happened next, I scanned another page of the diary, but the only reference to Perdita said that she'd had her disrupted trip to the hairdresser. Chatwell wrote a brief account of a long meeting he had had with his Logistics Officer, Basil Singleton, discussing a variety of ways in which JEEP might give practical assistance to journalists coming on exchange visits from the continent. When I turned another page, however, I saw that the next day's entry was a long one. Chatwell noted that he was making his usual daily quick scan of the *Financial Times* when

a sub-heading in a diary column caught my eye. It said, 'Canada Move', and the paragraph quoted a 'usually reliable source' which predicted that 'controversial journalist' Tom Wells was about to depart for Canada. He had not only secured a top job in the media company 'Voice and Vision Accadia', but was also about to marry the company's joint owner, Letitia Mackintosh, 'socialite and savvy business tycoon.' The columnist commented that his move would come as no surprise to those who knew him well, since his professional success had been matched by his accomplishments as a charmer of the opposite sex.

Hesitated for a moment about bringing the story to Perdita's attention, but this clearly wasn't idle gossip and she was bound to find out sooner or later. So I gave her a buzz and asked her to come to my office. I fear I had under-estimated the poor girl's fragility. When she read the piece her cheeks went pale, and then she opened her mouth and uttered a sound that I've heard before – a kind of despairing wail, but loud and uninhibited. And then she started to cry.

I moved around the desk to stand behind her chair, and handed her my usual large, white hankie. Said something like: 'Let it all come out. Deception is a cruel thing, but once you're able to think calmly again you'll maybe think it's better to be rid of the deceiver sooner rather than later.'

She sobbed for several minutes, and I went around the desk and stood behind her chair, holding her lightly by the shoulders. I asked if she'd like to go home and be alone, but she said she'd rather get on with her work and "forget about the bastard". She got up and went back to her own office.

His next reference to Perdita was in the following day's entry, where he commented, "Perdita seems to have recovered but didn't communicate much today." In a later entry he recorded that Perdita had told him she planned to spend the weekend at her parents' home, and he thought that was probably a good idea.

On the following Monday Perdita told him she'd had a row with her mother at the weekend. When he asked the reason she said it was because she'd been reading a book about lesbianism. "I'd talked about becoming a lesbian once before," she'd said, "but then it was only to annoy her. Now I'm thinking about it seriously."

I wondered if Chatwell had felt the same shock of disbelief as I did when I read those words. If he did then he didn't record it, but simply wrote, "Had a talk with Basil about increase in air fares."

Before I could turn to what happened next my telephone rang. To my surprise and delight it was Judith. She was ringing, she said, to check if I would be having my usual consultation with her next Friday. When I said that I would she went on, "I just wanted to get in first with an invitation to lunch, but reminding you that I'm going to pay this time. But I'd like to go back to the Piccolo, if that's OK with you. It would be very convenient for me – as well as being very nice."

I was more than happy to confirm the arrangement. It was the first time that a woman had taken the initiative in a relationship with me.

10

Giovanni welcomed us to the Café Piccolo as if we were regular diners (and I hoped that we very soon would be). I thought that Judith seemed pleased to be recognized by him. He recommended the 'maccheroni alla carbonara' and we were both pleased to settle for it. As we awaited its arrival Judith asked, "Do you think Theresa May is going to get the extension that she's asked for?"

I hadn't realized that she was interested in politics. "The commentators that I've read seemed to think she will," I replied. "I expect we'll know the answer tomorrow. There was an interesting article last Sunday about how Brexit has been dividing the country, with bitter arguments even inside families."

"That could include my family," said Judith, "except that our arguments aren't bitter. We just politely disagree. My father and I are Remainers but my brother is in favour of Brexit. He argues that because the EU is essentially protectionist it is preventing freer trade that would benefit a lot of poorer countries."

"I think he's broadly correct in that argument," I said, "even though I wasn't in favour of Brexit. I would have liked to see more realistic attempts by Britain to work with other EU countries that were against protectionism and centralization. What about your mother? Does she go along with your father?"

"Mum isn't really interested in politics. She was annoyed when some Brussels regulation meant that the plumber couldn't put a new central heating boiler where she wanted it to be; so I think that may have made her sympathetic to Brexit. But I don't think she voted in the referendum."

At that point our maccaroni arrived and conversation was suspended for a few minutes. Having enjoyed, and commented on, the food, I then asked, "Did you see Laura Kuensberg's TV programme – I think it was on Monday last week? She was claiming to be able to tell the 'inside story' of Brexit."

"I watched it with Henrietta and Georgina," she replied. "I didn't think it told us very much that we didn't already know. Georgina believes there's going to be a second referendum and people will change their minds, now that they can see what a terrible mess it has all become. Her father is a Liberal Democrat borough councillor."

"For that to happen, I'm sure there would have to be a general election first, and can you see Mrs May making that mistake a second time?" I said. "Talking of television programmes, did you see the one on Rembrandt last night?"

"Oh, yes. I thought it was brilliant. I'm looking forward to the next one in the series. Rembrandt is one of my favourite artists."

Her response raised the possibility of making some further progress, and I said, "He's one of mine, too. Because my parents have been living in the Netherlands in recent years I've had some good opportunities to look at his pictures. It was quite a thrill to visit the Rembrandt House and see the place where he did a lot of his work. But have you seen his pictures in the Wallace Collection?"

"No, I've never got around to that," she replied. "I'd love to see them."

"Would you like to go there with me one Saturday afternoon, and maybe we could have a meal together afterwards?" I suggested, studying her face to see what her reaction might be.

She seemed to be genuinely pleased, and instantly responded, "Oh yes, I'd like to do that. I'm afraid it can't be this Saturday, because I've arranged to spend the weekend at home with my parents, and mum wouldn't be pleased. It would be the second time I've postponed my visit."

"Of course – you mustn't upset her," I said, "especially if you're not going to be there at Easter. I'm planning to do my trip to meet journalists on the Continent in the week after Easter. It'll be pretty hectic, but I think I can visit six countries in seven days if I get the right connections."

"You won't have much time to see any interesting places, will you?" she observed. "Are you trying to maximise the number of interviews you can do within the budget?"

"That's exactly the reason," I replied, "But I hope I'll be able to squeeze in a few places of interest. No interview is going to last for more than a couple of hours. I'd particularly like to have a look around places where I might not go again – Krakow and Prague and Calais. I expect a lot will depend on how hospitable my interviewees are."

"I'll look forward to hearing about it when you get back," she said.

"And I'll look forward to telling you about it – and I'll try not to bore you. But thinking again about our visit to the Wallace, there's one picture there, apart from the Rembrandts, that I'd really like to look at with you. You've probably seen it in reproductions. It's the big Reubens called 'The Rainbow Landscape'."

"I think I have seen it reproduced," she said. "It's very different from a lot of his other pictures. They tend to be full of mythological ladies with big breasts."

I laughingly agreed. "The difference might be because he'd just settled down with his second, very young, wife when he painted it. One reason I like it, I think, is because it was painted by a man who was happy, and his happiness somehow comes across to you. Maybe that's a bit fanciful, but he never sold the picture and it must have been painted for his own pleasure."

"And maybe for his wife's pleasure, too," Judith observed.

"That's quite probable," I said. "Oh, you maybe know the other one that he painted around the same time, because it's in the National Gallery. It's really the other half of the same wide landscape, and it shows his new house, Het Steen. By all accounts he was very happy there, in a kind of semi-retirement."

"Oh, I think I do know that one," she said. "There's a little detail of a man shooting quail – is that the one?"

"Yes, it is. Constable was supposed to have been greatly influenced by looking at it."

"I think you're right about how the mood of the artist when he painted a picture can come across to you when you're looking

54

at it," she said. "I hope you'll have time to see some interesting ones on your trip."

"One of my stops is going to be in Haarlem and I shall definitely visit the Frans Halsmuseum."

"Doesn't he have a very famous picture in the Wallace?" she asked.

"Of course – the so-called 'Laughing Cavalier'. We must have a look at that and see what we make of it. Is he really laughing?"

She smiled and said, "I'm really looking forward to going there with you." At that point we were ready to choose a dessert. Judith opted for granita and I had cassata. She was concerned about getting back to the office on time and so we ate it quite quickly while Giovanni brought us espresso coffees that didn't detain us for long.

On the walk back to the office she told me that her prospects for promotion were looking good. Yesterday Mr George had made some encouraging remarks. I said, jokingly, that I must make sure I wasn't late in delivering any copy, so that her reputation wouldn't be damaged by having recommended me.

Before she turned into Portland Place I kissed her lightly on the left cheek and we went our separate ways. I felt as happy as Reubens might have been when he was painting his picture.

11

The following morning, still feeling euphoric after my successful lunch with Judith, I began working on plans for the short 'continental tour' for which financial provision had been made in Bodley's bequest. Trawling through articles written in the later years of JEEP I identified locations where there might still be people who remembered being involved in the scheme. From a list of eight possibilities I could see the potential for a tour that would begin in Belgium and the Netherlands, taking me into Germany, Denmark and Poland and returning via Prague, Vienna and Paris. Once potential interviewees had been identified I sent off a series of emails and hoped that at least some of them would evoke replies.

By the time I had completed this activity it was nearly three o'clock, and I went to the fridge in search of a quick snack to stave off hunger until the evening. A Marks and Spencer pork pie was still within sell-by date, and with the addition of a slightly soft tomato and the few remaining leaves of an Iceberg lettuce it provided me with what I needed.

When I had eaten I didn't feel like returning to serious work and decided instead to continue reading Winston Chatwell's increasingly interesting account of private relationships in the offices of JEEP. As I opened the volume containing a projecting Daunt's bookmark to remind me where I had left off I recalled how Perdita had been threatening to experiment with lesbianism, and wondered how long that despairing reaction to disappointment was going to last. Under February 22 Chatwell returned to the subject:

> *Perdita told me she was going to Oxford at the weekend, to meet a girl with whom she'd been to school. They had almost lost touch because, after school her friend, Melanie, had gone to Oxford while she had studied at Cambridge. Now Melanie was completing a PhD at Somerville and was*

earning a reputation as a contributor to lesbian periodicals. Perdita didn't say why the acquaintance was being renewed, but I assumed it must be related to her earlier statement about her sexuality. She then went on to say that she was having a bad time with her period, but expected it would be over by the weekend. I asked if she often had difficult periods (she hadn't mentioned the problem before) and she replied that she did. And she went on to say that going on the Pill might help but she didn't want to do that because of the risks. At the end of the afternoon, in response to my enquiry, she said she was feeling a little better.

In the next few diary entries there was no further reference to Perdita. On the Thursday and Friday Chatwell was busy with meetings on financial matters; and his weekend entries were characteristically brief, mentioning a long walk across Regent's Park, as far as the Zoo. On the following Monday, however, she featured prominently.

When Perdita brought in the post she was in a very cheerful mood. I asked how the weekend had gone and she replied, "Very interesting and very useful." She went on to say that Melanie would be coming to London next weekend, and added, "But I've got to be careful not to encourage her too much. It wouldn't be fair. I don't actually find her very attractive – she's put on a lot of weight since school. But I did learn a lot that was useful." And she gave one of her mischievous little smiles. When she was leaving I gave her a quick shoulder hug and she responded with an affectionate glance.

Perdita wasn't mentioned again in the diary until the Friday of that week, when she came to Chatwell's room to translate an article that had been sent by a Ligurian newspaper. When the work had been done Chatwell commented that she seemed to want to talk, and went on:

I asked if her linguistic ability had been evident when she was a child and she said she'd had the advantage of spending her early years in Switzerland, when her father was working in a bank in Zurich. At primary school she'd been virtually bilingual with German – but Swiss-German; and she'd also learned French in school. When I asked why she hadn't majored in German in her Modern Languages degree she said that wouldn't have been much of a challenge. Her father had come back to work in London when she was twelve, and she was sent to boarding-school.

She went on to say she'd had a row with her mother on the phone the previous evening, but she didn't at first say what was the reason for it. She'd been having headaches, and thought that suppressing her feelings might be causing them. And then she told me the row with her mother had been because she'd mentioned the meeting with her friend, Melanie, who was known to be a lesbian, and her mother had thought she was being seduced into homosexuality. But if there was any seducing she was the one who was doing it, she said.

The conversation then somehow got on to behaviourist psychology and the use of aversion therapy – to which she was very averse. After that we were speculating about whether all aesthetic appreciation has its origins in sexual desire and the biological need to ensure that mating instincts are powerful enough to get us into bed. At the end of the conversation she said she was feeling more relaxed. And then she revealed that she was planning to visit a lesbian club in Kensington on Saturday.

I asked what the club was called and she said "The Lonely Well". I guessed that the name must be derived from "The Well of Loneliness". She confirmed that it was, and that she had started reading the book. Told her that I had tried it once but had found it boring. She said she was feeling nervous about going to the club on her own, but felt it was something she had to do to test herself. I hoped – but didn't say so – that it might turn her off the idea of being bisexual.

Eager to see what the outcome of her visit to the club had been, I continued to turn the diary pages. In the next two working days Chatwell spent most of his time interviewing journalists, and at the weekend seemed to have gone out only once, apart from a visit to Waitrose. However, the Monday entry did not disappoint me.

Chatwell recorded that Perdita seemed eager to talk, after they had gone through the post together. Before long she told him about her visit to "The Lonely Well".

Perdita said she'd enjoyed her visit to the club, and had quickly lost her nervousness. I didn't want to seem inquisitive and refrained from asking questions, but it looked as if she must have been accompanied by Melanie, for she then told me she'd spent the night at Melanie's home, and her friend's mother had given them a room with a double bed. She went on to mention that at the club a nurse had pursued her very actively but she hadn't found her attractive. "Too butch for my liking," she said.

On Friday she had mentioned that she liked having something 'different and undemanding' to read to help her get to sleep at night. I brought her my copy of James Stephens' "The Crock of Gold" and that seemed to please her, and I was allowed to give her a hug. Then, for no particular reason, she started to talk about jealousy, and what an unpleasant characteristic it was. Melanie, she said, had been jealous when she'd talked to anyone else at the club. You only had a right to be jealous if someone had actually made a commitment to you, she went on, and I agreed. Suggested that maybe she needed to think carefully about her relationship with Melanie.

The rest of the week's diary entries were brief, and dominated by preparing for and having a meeting with someone from Brussels who was visiting London for talks at the Foreign Office. The visitor, a German by nationality, was enthusiastic about JEEP's plans and volunteered to help with contacts. There were a couple of brief references to 'friendly chat' with Perdita, but no new developments. Unsurprisingly, the following Monday brought new revelations, when Perdita reported on another visit to "The Lonely Well", this time on her own.

Perdita said that at the club the nurse, whose name is Dorothy, had made a "strong play" for her, but she had firmly declined her advances. Then she had met a Danish woman, who had really interested her in a disturbing kind of way. She was the representative in England for a company which made jewellery and metal sculptures, and her name was Ingrid. At the end of the evening Ingrid had invited Perdita to go home with her. Before that happened Perdita had been dancing with her and had said to her: "I'd like to make love to you." Everything had then happened very quickly. They had gone to Ingrid's flat and were very soon in bed together.

> *"Actually we wanted to do different things, but eventually it worked out all right," she said. The next day they had gone to an exhibition together and then back to bed.*

> *She was so full of delight that I said, "I'm glad you've got what you wanted." And I gave her a kiss on the top of her head, which she seemed to like.*

At the end of the afternoon Perdita had come to his office, wanting to talk.

> *She said she was beginning to have doubts about the gay scene, because it had such an artificial, hothouse atmosphere. Anyhow she was going home to her own flat this evening and would be able to think about things more clearly. I gave her a little hug around the shoulders when she was leaving, and she smiled at me very sweetly.*

A phone call from the editor ended my reading of the diary for that day.

12

The week that followed was a busy one. It included tidying up the arrangements for my European 'tour', which I was well pleased to be able to fit into a period in May. That meant I should be able to finish writing up the results of the interviews by the end of the month, and early completion of the book would be a possibility.

On the Friday I rang Judith, ostensibly to wish her well for her weekend trip to see her parents, and we chatted for about twenty minutes. She was envious of my European travel plans, and I made a mental note to propose a joint holiday trip when the moment seemed ripe. Jokingly I promised to send her a postcard.

The phone call put me in a mood to find out more about the evolving love life of Perdita, and so I turned once again to Chatwell's diary. The next entry in which her name appeared was on a Friday, and she announced that she was going to move in with Ingrid "for about half the time every week." Chatwell asked her whether she thought this arrangement would really be workable.

Perdita replied that it was a compromise. Ingrid had wanted her to give up her flat and move in with her permanently. "What she really wants is a marriage, and yet she was encouraging me to go out with the Malaysian girl I chatted with at the club. I'm not sure if she was testing me; and I'm not sure if I really want to be monogamous."

She went on to say she thought it was her affectionate nature that attracted people to her. I said her attractiveness gave her power to make people either happy or miserable, and so responsibility went along with it. She admitted that she had made Melanie, who had found out about the relationship, very miserable, but said the latter would get over it, because she was essentially promiscuous.

The following Monday's entry inevitably contained a report on Perdita's weekend.

> *She told me about another intense evening, and night, with Ingrid, who had promised to buy her a ring if they were still together at Christmas. It seemed that 'marriage' was the only kind of relationship that would satisfy her, but Perdita had serious doubts about Ingrid's possessiveness.*

In the afternoon Chatwell had another conversation with Perdita as she was preparing to leave. She told him she had called off a theatre outing that she'd arranged with the Malaysian girl, and asked him if he thought she'd done the right thing. He wrote:

> *I said she had (though it might have been more in my own interest for her to do the 'wrong thing'.) When she said she would really have liked to have the Malaysian as well I told her she was a greedy girl, and gave her a hug around her shoulders. She giggled happily, and actually snuggled against me for a moment.*

The next substantial reference to Perdita was on the Monday of the next week, when she didn't turn up for work. Chatwell recorded:

> *She rang about ten to say she'd been very sick at the weekend. It sounded like flu – aches and a slight fever. I was sympathetic but had to ring off because of an incoming call. I rang her back at lunchtime, when she said she was feeling better.*

Advised her to see a doctor, keep warm and stay off alcohol but drink a lot. She said she hoped she'd be much better tomorrow and would come to work if she was. Told her I'd love to see her, but not to come unless she felt really better. She surprised me by asking if we could have lunch together and of course I agreed.

On the following day the lunch duly took place and led to another of Chatwell's increasingly long entries.

As we walked to 'Il Portico' she told me she was feeling much better, but was suffering from a heavy period. Lack of sleep and lack of privacy had exacerbated the illness, she thought; and she agreed with my suggestion that it might be good to go back to her own flat for a few days. Lack of peace and quiet was the main cause of dissatisfaction with her present way of living, she said.

Over lunch she mentioned that Melanie's aggressiveness towards her had upset her a lot. I suggested that it wasn't unusual for someone who had been bitterly disappointed in a relationship to become aggressive towards the former object of their love, and she agreed. On the way back she asked me to go with her into Boots to buy a face pack, and I did. Back at the office I gave her a little hug and she rewarded me with a very affectionate smile. Wonder if her illness could be psychosomatic.

In the next day's entry Chatwell, after describing two long business meetings in the morning and early afternoon, said:

When we got together at the end of the day Perdita was bursting to tell me what had happened with Ingrid yesterday and today. Last night Ingrid had wanted to make love when they went to bed, but she had been just too tired. However, they planned to have a long weekend, and she asked if she could have Friday off. I said she could – trying not to show my reluctance.

The Thursday entry recorded that Perdita phoned to say she had slept in after a very late night. He wrote:

For once I was strong-minded and said I was sorry but I needed her to translate some material that had arrived in the post from Italy. When she came she said she had been happy to come, but it was Ingrid who had suggested she stay at home. I asked why she hadn't told Ingrid that she had a terribly strict boss, and she replied, "Unfortunately she already knows that I haven't." I gave her a quick hug. Later she told me about their holiday plans, which involve a lot of motoring. We were standing side by side when she was leaving, and she gave me a little hug, saying, "Thank you for being so understanding."

Not unsurprisingly, the next substantial entry in the diary was on the following Monday. Perdita was back from her weekend break, and Chatwell wrote:

She was at her desk when I arrived, looking bright-eyed and better than for some time. The holiday had been enjoyable, she said; but Ingrid had been very demanding of her time, making it impossible to read a book, or just be quiet. She was starting to think the relationship couldn't last.

*I encouraged her to think that Ingrid might be open
to making changes if she was really so
desperately keen on her. Suggested it would be
appropriate to spend some time in her own flat
now, and she agreed.*

*Took her to the Portico for lunch and she told
me more details of the holiday. Ingrid needed
constant reassurance, she said, and also seemed
to want to tell her about all her past lovers –
something she found it difficult to understand. On
our way back to the office I lent her money to buy
mascara at Boots. When we parted at her office
door she gave me a light kiss on the cheek. Felt
euphoric for the rest of the afternoon.*

Chatwell had to spend most of Tuesday in meetings and had only
one brief encounter with Perdita. She told him that on the previous
evening she and Ingrid had met with a Danish lesbian couple who
were planning to open a club in London; and they had had too
much to drink. She was feeling a little hungover. The Friday entry
quickened my interest.

*When we were going through the post together
Perdita suddenly announced, "I'm going to leave
Ingrid. I can't stand the strain for much longer."
Advised her that, if she did make a break, she
should choose her time carefully. At lunchtime a
friend from her university days, an American girl
called Fenella, came, and they went off to the
Portico together. At the end of the afternoon she
looked into my office and said that she'd changed
her mind about leaving Ingrid. She'd been telling
Fenella about Ingrid, and although her friend is
'straight' she'd been full of admiration for Ingrid's
sexuality. It had made her think again, and so
she'd decided to give the relationship more time to
develop. As she was leaving she kissed me lightly*

*on the cheek and I returned the kiss. Not sure
what to think.*

The next Monday's entry was a continuation of the on-off story.

*Perdita was late in arriving and missed the staff
meeting. She looked a little dishevelled, and I
invited her into my office to talk. As I suspected,
there had been a great emotional upset with
Ingrid, who had been quite hysterical. Although
she still wants to leave, Perdita said she was
reluctant, partly because she feels sorry for Ingrid
and partly because the sex is good.*

*Took her to lunch at the Portico and bought
her a glass of red wine. We talked mainly about
her dilemma, and I tried to reassure her that she
had nothing to feel guilty about, and should follow
her own inclinations. On the way back bought a
Portuguese dictionary for her to use in translating
a long article from a Lisbon paper that arrived
yesterday. She was confident that her knowledge
of Italian and Latin would enable her to cope with
it; and by the end of the afternoon she had done a
complete translation. By way of reward I kissed
her cheek and she returned the kiss.*

*She said she was dreading the evening,
because she was going to have to tell Ingrid that
she was moving out permanently tomorrow
morning. Maybe it was the beginning of her period
that had helped her to think more rationally about
the sexual desire element in the relationship, she
added. She wondered why everyone she'd had a
relationship with – apart from a married man –
had eventually needed her too much, and she'd
had to step away from it. I said she'd probably
been unlucky; and it wasn't unusual for younger*

people to want a relationship that was permanent. As she was leaving I hugged her around the shoulders and kissed her cheek, hoping that all would go well.

The drama continued on Tuesday, when Chatwell wrote:

Perdita arrived late, carrying a large suitcase. I told her to go into my room, and brought her a large coffee. She said it had been a dreadful evening, with lots of tears and recriminations. Finally, to appease Ingrid she had agreed to spend two nights a week with her.

When she'd finished the coffee she said she was feeling cold and so I moved a chair and sat beside her, hugging her tightly. "That's nice," she said, and I kissed her cheek. I suggested she should give herself a whole week on her own to sort out her feelings, and she agreed.

I noticed a red mark on her neck and she said it was a love bite that Ingrid had given her. We talked about love bites and she told me about early boyfriends who had bitten – or refused to bite her. Once she had admonished a boy, saying it would make her "look like a shopgirl" if she had bite marks. "That was very snobbish of you," I said, and she agreed, giggling. She went on to say that in her teens she had been very serious, but had become totally relaxed at Cambridge, somewhat to the dismay of her mother.

The she said that unexpectedly her period pains had recurred, and I urged her to consult a doctor if they persisted. I then had to leave her for an appointment with a London NUJ representative. That encounter went well, and he invited me to address a branch meeting next month.

Later in the afternoon worked on some letters to France and Belgium with Perdita. We sat side by side at my desk. She was planning to have her hair cut at the weekend, and we discussed styles that would suit her. When she said that my advice was always good I put my hand on her thigh and gently squeezed. The well-worn blue denim was soft to the touch and the flesh which it covered was firm and resilient. To my amazement I discovered that I was having an erection. I removed my hand and she smiled in a way that I could only describe as 'conspiratorial', saying she had better be getting ready to leave, as she had a lot to do this evening. As she stood up to go I noticed the label on the back of her jeans, just below the belt. The brand name was 'Heaven', and I reflected (to myself) that the makers had chosen a very appropriate description.

My stomach reminded me that it was time to have something to eat, and I closed the diary with the thought that it was becoming a much more intriguing read than I had ever expected it to be.

13

The Easter weekend passed uneventfully. Judith was visiting her parents, and I needed time to make preparations for my European trip. The weather was fine and I had a long walk through Regent's Park and another from Green Park to St James's. And I treated myself to a lunch at the Caffé Piccolo. On the Wednesday I set off on my trip to interview journalists who could still remember their contacts with JEEP.

To make sure that Judith didn't forget me, and to provide an easy introduction to the suggestion of a future holiday together, I had decided to send her a picture postcard, with a light-hearted message, from each of the places that I visited. In Ghent I was in two minds about sending a card depicting, surprisingly, the Brussels 'Manneken-Pis', but decided against it, realizing that I was not yet familiar enough with her sense of humour. So I settled for the safe option of a view of Sint Baafskathedraal.

My next stop was Haarlem, where the obvious choice was a picture of the Frans Halsmuseum. With the help of the excellent Dutch railway system I was able to spend that night with my parents in Delft before moving on to Aachen next day. There I had a friendly reception from an editor who remembered attending, as a young journalist, a London seminar organized by JEEP in 1999. After our conversation he insisted on taking me in his little Volkswagen to see the legendary Karlschrein in the cathedral. A picture of Charlemagne's marble throne was on the card that I posted to Judith.

The next lap of the journey was not so relaxing, involving a flight to Warsaw and a long train journey to Krakow. In that city I met two journalists who had had contact with JEEP, one as an editor and the other as a reporter who visited Cambridge in 1999. I had time for a quick visit to Wawel, with its Royal Cathedral and Castle, before trudging wearily to a hotel for food and a good night's sleep. The card for Judith had a picture of the golden-domed Sigismund Chapel.

Next day I boarded a train for Prague, where I had an interview with the only woman journalist that I met on the trip.

She was now a television presenter, but had visited Birmingham as a young journalist in 2001. I had time to visit the Old Town Hall and the incredible Astronomical Clock and have a quick look at the legendary Charles Bridge (which featured on my postcard) before leaving for the airport.

The flight to Paris was quick, but it was followed by a tedious train journey to Calais, where I arrived just in time to have supper before subsiding into bed. My interview next morning was with an editor who was more interested in talking about Brexit than about his attachment to a Kent newspaper some twenty years earlier. He treated me to lunch, and I then paid a visit to Rodin's sculpture of the Burghers of Calais. It was the subject of my chosen postcard, and I wrote, "What about having a look at the other version, in the Victoria Tower Gardens – maybe one Saturday afternoon?"

I crossed the Channel by ferry that evening, and was happy to get to sleep again in my own bed. When I was having breakfast next morning the telephone rang and, much to my delight, it was Judith. She asked how the trip had gone, and thanked me for the cards from Ghent and Haarlem. The others had not yet arrived. We talked for about ten minutes and then she said she would have to be leaving for work. I asked if she would like to go on Saturday afternoon to an exhibition at the British Library on "Writing" and received an enthusiastic "Yes." So I said I'd ring again later in the week to settle the details, and returned to my breakfast feeling hugely elated.

The rest of the day was spent in writing up the findings of my trip. They added some colour, if not very much substance, to the conclusions I had drawn from the written material. I felt it would not be appropriate for me to express personal opinions in the book; but I had reached the conclusion that JEEP had probably had very little influence on EU-UK relationships, although it had been valuable professionally to many of the participants.

After enjoying a cottage pie I had been keeping in the freezer since my last venture into home cooking I had decided to pass the time before going to bed by having another look at the unfolding story of Chatwell and Perdita. Taking up the story from where I had prudently inserted a bookmark in the diary, I found that Perdita was now in a quiet mood, having decided she was going to try to keep the relationship with Ingrid on an even keel, at least until they had had a holiday together in Denmark, which they were currently planning. So, for the next three weeks Chatwell's references to her were brief, although they included a couple of occasions when he gave her a hug after some minor mishap. Then, in the middle of June, she went off with Ingrid for a fortnight's holiday, and diary entries reverted to being brief and telegraphic.

The entry for Monday, July 2nd, was a lot longer. Chatwell wrote:

> *Hoped Perdita would come in, and she did. When we were alone I hugged her tightly and kissed her cheek. She had a lot to tell about the holiday. Apart from two days spent in Copenhagen it seems to have consisted mainly of visiting all of Ingrid's boorish relations, over-eating and over-drinking with them and hearing about their convoluted relationships and their narrow, bourgeois (in the worst sense of the word) ambitions. She didn't seem to have enjoyed it.*
>
> *Before going home in the afternoon she came and had tea with me. She talked about Ingrid starting to get fat, and said she didn't really mind that, because there was something nice about having more flesh to fondle. I concurred, and briefly put my hand on her thigh and gave a little fondle.*

On the following day, after recounting plans for a "Best Euro Journalist" competition, Chatwell wrote:

> *Perdita looked tired this morning. Asked her if anything was the matter and she said she'd had an argument in bed with Ingrid, about relative amounts of space occupied. In the afternoon she*

made tea and came to sit beside me and talk. I put my hand on her thigh and after a time she removed it, saying it was hot. Then she realized the heat was from her mug of tea, resting on her other thigh, and my hand was allowed to go back. When she got up to leave she said, "I'm supposed to be a homosexual, you know." I responded, "But you still feel like a woman," and she laughed and blew me a kiss as she went out.

The Friday entry included another conversation with Perdita, in which she talked about plans to go to a ball in Salisbury on the following day – with Ingrid, of course. She said that the outfit Ingrid had chosen for the occasion made her look very masculine.

Needless to say, she reported back on the following Monday. The ball hadn't been an unqualified success. Ingrid had become "slightly tipsy", and while trying to stand on a table to see some belly dancers had collapsed among the wine bottles. She had then become sulky when Perdita had declined to join her in a "rather enthusiastic dance". So they had finally packed up and driven home through the night, faster than was prudent.

Next day Ingrid had called, by arrangement, at lunchtime, to take Perdita to see a short play at the Arts Theatre. Chatwell wrote:

She was shorter, and older-looking than I'd expected – hyperactive, with a very attractive, vulnerable smile. Maybe it was because I already knew her orientation, but she had a slightly masculine air which for me cancelled out her sexiness.

When I had tea with Perdita in the afternoon I gave her my impressions, and she said she thought Ingrid "repressed consciousness of her own sexiness" – which puzzled me. She went on to say that if ever she left Ingrid she might take up with Dorothy, whom she still saw at the club sometimes. The only problem was that she'd heard some people say that Dorothy was frigid, and she wouldn't be able to make love to someone who didn't respond.

She went on to say that Ingrid was constantly reviling men, saying that all they wanted was somewhere to poke it. "She accuses me of being an extrovert, and also of being puritanical. Actually, I think I have strong maternal feelings, and that's how I sometimes feel towards Ingrid. I want to take her on my knee and stroke her – but she's too big for that." I said that nobody was too big for that, and she laughed and said it was time for her to be going home.

On the following day Chatwell took Perdita to lunch at the 'Il Portico' restaurant. Again she began talking about the possibility of leaving Ingrid, and said that she hated the idea of being owned by – or of owning – anybody. Chatwell wrote:

I strongly concurred with that sentiment. She went on to express some misgivings about the 'gay scene', saying she was just beginning to discover how complex it was, and adding that when her relationship with Ingrid was over she might avoid it for a while.

On our way back to the office we went into Metyclean and I bought her a portable typewriter, using £25 I'd been given as a fee for writing a book review. Then she said she needed to buy a pair of knickers, and we discussed what kind she liked on the way to the shop. I made a mental note for possible use in the future. When we finally got back I was allowed to kiss both her cheeks and

give her a hug around the waist. I couldn't resist
thinking about future possibilities.

Entries over the next week, however, had only minimal references to Perdita, and Chatwell seemed to be busy preparing to go on holiday. He departed on the Sunday, for Switzerland, and diary entries for the next fortnight were telegraphic in their brevity, and probably written up after his return. He went first to Vitznau, on Lake Lucerne, using it as a base for excursions every day to places in that region. Then he moved to Interlaken, in the Bernese Oberland, and used it similarly for excursions – mainly to the tops of mountains. One entry in particular caught my eye. He wrote:

Up to Grindelwald by the familiar train. Stayed for
only a couple of hours. The memories were too
poignant. On return walked to Boenigen along lake
shore and back via Wilderswil.

I guessed that he might, perhaps, have spent a holiday in that village with his late wife – maybe even their honeymoon – and the memories of their happiness turned to sadness. It was the only hint of emotion in the holiday diary entries. At that point I inserted the bookmark, closed the notebook and went to bed.

14

On Saturday my visit to the British Library with Judith to see the exhibition that was appropriately entitled "Writing" was a success, and we were mutually fascinated by the themes that it explored. However, my hope that she might afterwards come home with me to have something to eat was dashed. Her mother had asked her to meet a cousin who was arriving on a flight from Canada at Heathrow that evening, and so she had to leave me. I wasn't too disappointed, because she seemed to have enjoyed my company – as I had enjoyed hers – and she enthusiastically accepted my suggestion for lunch together after our next professional consultation, which was due on the coming Wednesday. We exchanged cheek kisses when we parted at the Tube station.

When I'd eaten my Scotch egg and salad I decided, as a kind of consolation, that I'd read some more of Chatwell's diaries. Having returned from his holiday, he went into work on the Monday morning and found that Perdita was already at her desk. He wrote:

I kissed her cheek, which she proferred willingly. But then she began to cry, and told me that she had left Ingrid. I took her into my room and heard the whole story. She had gone out one evening with her American friend, Fenella, and they had had a few drinks. On her return Ingrid had quizzed her in a jealous way, and it made her feel trapped. So she had left, but now she was feeling that she might have been selfish, and she'd agreed to meet Ingrid that evening.

In the afternoon, when we were working on translations, she complained of flashing in front of her eyes, a migraine symptom. I made her sit in the shade and covered her face with my handkerchief, and later I massaged her shoulders.

*That seemed to relieve the tension. I offered no
advice for her encounter this evening, although I
think she would be better to stick with the
separation. Work was much interrupted but I did
manage to catch up fairly well.*

Not surprisingly, Chatwell returned to the same topic in the
following day's entry:

*Perdita very late this morning. Could see she was
distressed when she came to my office. I stood up
and hugged her tightly, kissing her cheek. Then I
made coffee and we sat and talked about the
meeting with Ingrid. She talked some more about
the break-up. I said that Ingrid seemed to be
someone she loved but didn't like, and she agreed.
She had made up her mind that she really was
leaving Ingrid. I suggested that she might think
now about all the things she hadn't been able to
do, and plan to do them.*

*She does seem determined to leave, but
knows her own weakness. We didn't have any
more time together. When she was leaving she
looked in at my door and I told her I'd be thinking
about her in the evening.*

The story continued next day, but Chatwell had first to talk to a
visiting news photographer, before he was able to go to Perdita's
office. He wrote:

*Found her looking distressed, and she
immediately burst into tears. Took her in my arms
and she held me very tightly. Ingrid had been
hysterical in her demands, saying she would do
anything to keep Perdita. So she'd spent the night*

*there, but she wanted to 'escape'. She sobbed on
my shoulder and I spoke to her comfortingly,
saying that if it was affecting her in this way she
ought to make the break. When she asked if she
could have two days off I said yes, but suggested
she come in tomorrow if she felt better. She
agreed, and said she would talk to me on the
phone. Told her that she didn't have to keep me
informed, but she said she wanted to.*

*In the afternoon Perdita phoned. Said that
Ingrid had telephoned, desperate to have her
back. I advised her to avoid having contact, saying
that would be being kind to Ingrid as well. Her
friend, Melanie, had invited her to Oxford for the
weekend, and I encouraged her to accept.*

On the following day Perdita didn't come into the office, but late
in the afternoon she telephoned. Chatwell wrote:

*She said she'd had an upset tummy, probably
because of anticipating a call from Ingrid. The call
had come after lunchtime and had been a painful
experience. She had been firm, saying that they
ought not to meet again, and then Ingrid had been
abusive, calling her a leech, and saying she didn't
want to see her around the gay scene again. I said
it might have been for the best that it ended on an
abrasive note because it had revealed the limits on
the relationship. Love that might be the basis of a
'marriage' could never include the kind of anger
that Ingrid had displayed, I suggested.*

*She said she'd decided not to go to Oxford
after all. Instead she was going to visit some
friends with her mother. Wished her well for the
weekend.*

Predictably, when I looked at the Monday diary entry I found that Perdita was thinking once again of changing her mind. Chatwell wrote:

> *Perdita told me she'd had a letter from Ingrid. It suggested that they could live apart but have an 'affair'; and Perdita was thinking that she might accept the offer, at least until they'd had a holiday together in Scotland which had already been planned. I decided to offer no more advice, except to suggest that a meeting they're going to have this evening should be on neutral ground, with no 'going home' afterwards, in either direction. She agreed, and came to me to be hugged, offering a cheek to be kissed.*

The next day's entry revealed that his advice had been taken. Ingrid had agreed to go ahead with the holiday, and Perdita had turned down an invitation to go home with her for the night. Chatwell gave her several congratulatory kisses. On the day after they had a long discussion about things she might do when in Scotland, and he offered to lend her a pair of binoculars. She revealed that she had a keen interest in butterflies and moths, which had begun when she was at school, studying biology. On his way home he bought a copy of a little Collins Gem Guide to Butterflies and Moths. Next day he presented it to Perdita, along with his binoculars.

> *Perdita's face lit up when I gave her the book. She threw her arms around my neck and kissed me on both cheeks, saying, "I love getting presents. This is going to get me really interested again."*

The diary entries for the next fortnight were brief, and Chatwell seemed to spend most of his time drafting proposals for an 'Exchange Journalist of the Year' award, and consulting about it with members of his Council. I knew all about it, because I had already written a chapter of the book outlining its development, and describing the annual presentation ceremonies, at which politicians or media heavyweights presented the awards. A file of the annual brochures had provided all the necessary information. On the Monday when Perdita returned a full page and a half were needed for the day's entry. He wrote:

When Perdita came to my room I took her in my arms and kissed her several times on the cheeks. She seemed to be in good heart but it was immediately evident that the holiday had not been a success. The weather had not been good, and Ingrid had displayed all her worst traits, to such an extent that Perdita had stopped feeling physically attracted to her. Even their parting from one another on Sunday had been acrimonious; but Perdita seemed relieved that it was really over. She appeared anxious to tell me everything about the holiday, and accepted an invitation to lunch at Il Portico.

Over lunch we talked a bit more about the holiday, and the disappointing scarcity of butterflies, probably because of the weather. She had forgotten to bring my binoculars, but promised to do so tomorrow. Then, surprisingly, she began to talk about her childhood, and how deliberately naughty and rebellious she'd been at school, especially between the ages of ten and thirteen. She thought it was only because she was outstanding academically that she wasn't expelled.

It was raining when we left the restaurant and we ran back together through the rain, stopping at Woolworth's on the way to buy some Darjeeling tea. When I was leaving her in her office she proferred her cheek to be kissed. A button on her blouse was unfastened and I said, teasingly, that I'd seen her St Christopher medal. "What else did you see?" she asked, and I replied, "Beautiful things." She laughed and said, "You make me feel better."

Before she went home there was a phone call from Ingrid. She came to tell me that it had been "calm but valedictory." I advised her to start thinking about all the nice things she would be able to do, now that she was free.

The following day's diary entry was uneventful. Perdita announced that she was thinking of joining a transcendental meditation class. And on the next day, when they were returning from a meeting at the TGWU and taking a detour through Dean's Yard she said she would like one day to go to Evensong in Westminster Abbey. Chatwell offered to accompany her and she accepted. On the Wednesday she told him that she'd had a valedictory letter from Ingrid, but it didn't change anything. Next day the mood changed again. Chatwell wrote:

When I got back to the office from talking to our travel agents Perdita came to see me. She'd had a phone call from Ingrid, who had been very distressed and wanted to see her, and she had agreed to meet her. I advised meeting in a public place, and maintaining a firm attitude. She agreed, but was anxious about being able to see it through.

In the afternoon she came to report. There had been a tearful scene but it had been sorted out. At first she'd conceded that they might meet again, somewhere, sometime. But Ingrid had gone on the offensive, trying to attribute blame, and so they had parted. I praised her firmness and kissed her cheek. And I reassured her that her feeling of relief at being out of a trap was perfectly natural.

The Friday entry was something of an anti-climax. Chatwell had to attend three meetings and saw Perdita only at the end of the day. He wrote:

She seemed to be in a contented mood, and was planning to visit her family at the weekend. When I gave her cheek a farewell kiss I thought I detected a slight withdrawal, but I might have been imagining it. I ought to stop hoping for the impossible.

15

My lunch with Judith went well. The copyright issues that day were all straightforward, and so she was able to leave the office early, enabling us to have a more leisurely meal. While we were waiting for the first course to arrive she asked, "Have you come across anything interesting in Mr Chatwell's diaries? You said you were working your way through them."

"An unusual story does seem to be developing," I replied. "It involves a young woman who worked for him. She was actually the niece of Bodley, the founder and patron of his organization. To describe her as 'sexually active' would be an understatement; and for some reason – maybe estrangement from her parents – she tells Chatwell all about her adventures, and he writes it down in the diaries. I think he might be attracted to her, because he's been a widower for some time. And in the period I'm reading about now she has decided to be a lesbian."

"I bet you didn't expect to find that in the diaries," said Judith. "Are you going to use any of it to add some spice to your volume of history?"

"Definitely not," I replied. "To use a phrase you must be familiar with, it would not be in the public interest. Of course, that doesn't mean the public wouldn't be interested. It never does. But as far as I'm concerned, it's just a glimpse that I'm being given of two people's private lives. If one of them was famous and I was writing the official biography that might be a different matter. But they're just private individuals and I think they should remain private, even though one of them, at least, is dead."

"I think you're right," she said. "I'd be surprised if Chatwell had written it all down with the expectation that anyone else was going to read it. They're not exactly in the same category as Prince Harry and Meghan. Did you see all the stories yesterday about their baby son? They seem to want to be private but have lots of publicity when they choose to."

"I expect the politicians were relieved to have attention diverted from the results of last week's local government elections. None of them had much to be happy about," I said.

"Do you think it might help Mrs May to get some kind of consensus on a Brexit agreement? They must all be worried about losing public support," she observed.

"I really don't know," I said. "I'm a bit out of touch with the political news after my travels; but I can't ever remember a time when Parliament was so unpredictable."

At that moment our risotto Genovese arrived (we'd both chosen the same first course) and for the next few minutes conversation was muted. I was pleased to see that Judith was eating enthusiastically and was evidently relaxed in my company. When the waiter was clearing the plates she said, "Oh, I forgot to tell you that your postcard from Calais arrived this morning. I would love to have a look at 'The Burghers of Calais' sculpture with you. I don't think I've ever seen it."

"Great!" I replied. "Shall we try this Saturday afternoon, and hope that the pro- and anti- Brexit demonstrators haven't closed the street? And maybe you'd like to come and have something to eat with me afterwards. I'm a reasonable cook, but with a limited menu."

When she replied, "That sounds like a nice idea," my hopes went soaring upward. For the first time we would be alone together in a private place, and she must have recognized the implications of that when she agreed. I quickly settled the details of time and place for our meeting, and she then questioned me about things I'd seen on my visit to Europe. She was particularly interested in Haarlem and I said, trying to sound casual, "Maybe some time we might go together to one of the candle-lit concerts they hold in Frans Hals's house."

To my delight she seemed to take the suggestion seriously, and responded, "What a super idea. I'd love to do that."

"We must put it on our agenda," I said. "Maybe it could be a celebration when I finish the manuscript. I'm hoping to hand it over to your boss in about a fortnight."

"On the day you do hand it over can I treat you to lunch to celebrate?" she asked. That, I told her, was the most welcome invitation that I'd ever had. She had to hurry back to her office when we'd finished our coffee; and I returned home 'walking on air'.

I felt too elated to settle down to work that afternoon, and so I decided to read some more of the diaries. Picking up the volume with the protruding bookmark, I wondered if Perdita had really left Ingrid for good. The next day was a Friday, and apart from telling Chatwell that her period had started unexpectedly during the night, she had nothing to report. However, in the late afternoon there was a phone call from Ingrid.

Afterwards she came to tell me about it. She confessed, a little hesitantly, that she'd been missing Ingrid – and she'd agreed to meet her this evening! I pretended not to be as astonished as I was, and counselled her against jumping into anything, suggesting that before the meeting she should think carefully about what she wanted to get out of it. Maybe she could try for a day-to-day approach, with no commitments that would make her feel trapped again. When she was leaving I hugged her and kissed her cheek, saying, "I hope it will go well."

I turned quickly to the next Monday entry, to discover what had happened. Perdita was late in arriving at work, but Chatwell saw at once that she was in a good mood. He wrote:

She told me there had been a reconciliation with Ingrid who had been much more reasonable, and they had spent the night together. She then began to talk about a quarrel she had had yesterday with her mother, and this brought tears to her eyes. We were sitting side by side, ostensibly checking the post, and she came into my arms for comfort quite spontaneously. I hugged her gently and kissed her forehead, and she soon recovered.

She asked whether I thought she would benefit from psychotherapy, and I didn't encourage the idea. To my surprise she said that feelings of guilt had played a strong part in her affair with Ingrid. I kissed her again on the cheek, but then we had to break off because the printer's representative had arrived to see me.

On the following day he recorded that Perdita had had a phone call from Ingrid and had come to his office to tell him about it.

She was a little upset because Ingrid had been brusque. I asked her if the reconciliation was really working, and she said she knew now that she wasn't really in love with Ingrid. I gave her a hug and told her that she shouldn't think she was to blame. Ingrid's attitude to her had displayed a lack of the kind of love that involves caring and tenderness. She agreed, saying that she thought tenderness was even more important than passion. Passion, I said, was something that could be switched on when you wanted it, but tenderness needed to be there all the time. Before she left I embraced her warmly again and she gave me a very affectionate glance before closing the door.

For the rest of the week there were only brief references to Perdita. She had caught a cold and had contact with Ingrid only on the telephone. Chatwell advised her to stay at home and nurse the cold on Friday, which she did. On Monday morning she was better and back at work. Chatwell wrote:

Once again she has decided to break with Ingrid. I think it might be a serious decision. She just can't stand the unsettled way of life. When she began to cry I went around the desk, held her in my arms and comforted her, kissing her gently. I tried to strengthen her resolution, because it's clear that the relationship isn't making her happy any longer. She became more cheerful as we talked; and then she began discussing other topics, like TV programmes she'd seen at the weekend.

In the afternoon her mind was still very much on the separation. When she was leaving I kissed her cheek and advised her to stick with her resolution.

At that point I had a phone call from my mother, and I didn't return to the diaries again that day. However, I thought about them as I was going to bed, and made a bet with myself that Perdita's separation from Ingrid wouldn't last for more than a fortnight.

16

Saturday proved to be a disappointment. I was showering when the telephone rang. The troubled voice of Judith told me that her mother had had a fall the evening before and was in hospital awaiting an X-ray. The doctor thought she had dislocated a tendon in her leg, but they wanted to have an X-ray to make sure there wasn't a fracture. So she was going to go home for the weekend – and she was really sorry about having to cancel our date. And from her tone of voice I thought that she really was.

I spent the morning working on an article about Gustavus Adolphus of Sweden for *Great Captains*. After lunch of pork pie and salad I walked across Regent's Park under a cloudy sky, reflecting on whether or not European history would have been very different if the Swedish king had not died at Lutzen in 1632. I wondered if there might be an 'alternative history' scenario to be written based on that hypothesis. When I got back home, however, I was in the mood for something lighter and decided to find out whether my prediction about Perdita's indecisiveness had been correct. So I opened the Chatwell diary volume with the bookmark.

Chatwell's first reference to Perdita was about having tea with her in the afternoon. They talked about an article on butterflies that she had been reading, but soon the conversation reverted to Ingrid.

She said she thought she had done the right thing, and went on to assert that it had been a different kind of relationship from any other that she had experienced. While we were talking the phone rang and it was Ingrid. I took the call and said that Perdita had gone on leave. Ingrid asked if she was at home and I replied that I didn't know, but it might be worth trying there. Perdita seemed pleased to have my complicity, and I seized the opportunity to kiss her cheek.

On the following day he was busy with a meeting of the Management Council. Herbert Bodley asked Chatwell how Perdita was getting on and he replied that she was fitting in very well and proving to be extremely useful. When the meeting was over Bodley visited Perdita in her office and had a brief chat with her. After his departure she went to see Chatwell, and he wrote that her mood was much more light-hearted than on the previous day.

Next day Perdita had a headache and Chatwell allowed her to go home after lunch. Ingrid rang again during the afternoon, and this time was "suspicious of conspiracy". He pretended not to understand what she was talking about, and then rang Perdita to tell her what had happened. On the following morning, as they were going through the post together, she told him she was thinking about going back with Ingrid. He wrote:

Apparently they had had an amicable phone conversation and Ingrid had not been abusive. She is hoping for a two days a week relationship. I encouraged her to make sure that Ingrid really understood what boundaries she wanted in the relationship, and she agreed. I urged her not to think that there was something wrong with herself, with her own attitudes.

At teatime she told me she was going to get in touch with the doctor who had treated her when she returned from Perugia. She is bothered about the heavy periods she has been having. I was sympathetic, and kissed her hand several times, which seemed to please her. Then she began to talk about the planned reconciliation with Ingrid this evening. Advised her to keep cool and try to give Ingrid time for second thoughts about any agreement they might make. When she was leaving she seemed nervous and I hugged her lightly and kissed her cheek.

In the following day's entry Chatwell said that Perdita looked happy on arrival at the office, and had said that things had gone well with Ingrid.

> *They had spent the night together – hence, I*
> *suppose the sparkle in her eyes. She came*
> *willingly to my arms for a hug and a kiss. Her talk*
> *was mainly about things they might plan to do*
> *together, and she asked me if I could get her*
> *information about times when National Trust*
> *properties are open (I'd mentioned that I'm on their*
> *mailing list). Twice during the conversation she*
> *stretched out a hand and touched my arm.*

On the following Monday Chatwell had several meetings, and his only mention of Perdita was to say that she seemed to be content. However, the contentment didn't last long. Two days later he wrote:

> *In the early afternoon Perdita had a call from*
> *Ingrid, and afterwards she told me about it. Ingrid*
> *hadn't wanted to go to the cinema tonight but had*
> *insisted that they should go if Perdita wanted to;*
> *and she had refused to let Perdita help with the*
> *housework. When she told me this she burst into*
> *tears, and I tried to comfort her by saying that*
> *Ingrid had probably been trying too hard to be*
> *nice. I made a cup of tea and she said she felt*
> *better. She asked me to sharpen her eyebrow*
> *pencil, and I presented it to her with a kiss on her*
> *cheek. Before going home she changed her blouse*
> *and put on make-up, and when I admired the*
> *result she allowed me to give her another kiss.*

The next entry said that Perdita had looked a little strained when she arrived at work.

She hadn't slept well, and thought that spending a third day with Ingrid was probably a mistake. Gave her a kipper paté sandwich for her lunch – I'd fancied having one myself and made a second in the hope that she would like it. We didn't have much talk because she had a slight toothache and asked to leave early.

On the day after Perdita didn't come in to work, going instead to the dentist. The story picked up again with the next Monday entry, which Chatwell prefaced with the remark, "A glorious autumn day".

Perdita seemed a little strained to begin with, but when we had finished the post she relaxed, and told me that she had arranged to see Doctor Lang, who had helped her when she came back from her year in Italy. Apparently he specializes in attending to students of some of the smaller London University colleges. She mentioned SOAS, Westfield and Bedford. He had been a friend of her mother when they were both students. His practice was in Wimpole Street, and I agreed to accompany her there on the Tube at lunchtime.

She went on to talk about her feelings of tension with Ingrid. I said it was a pity they weren't both able to accept the limitations on what they wanted from each other. At lunchtime, when I left her at Wimpole Street I had a quick walk in the southern end of Regent's Park, admiring the autumnal colours of the trees, before returning to the office.

It was mid-afternoon before Perdita got back, and she came to my office straight away. Doctor Lang had been sympathetic, she said, and had

*advised that she ought to see a psychotherapist –
possibly someone at the Tavistock Clinic. She
seemed inclined to take his advice. Her greatest
difficulty, she thought, was her inability to become
deeply involved with any one person – either a
man or a woman. I marvelled at her willingness to
be so open with me, and she said that was
something that was fairly new. I said I didn't think
she was in the least neurotic, and when she wept
it was just a natural safety valve. In my opinion
she didn't "need" to see a therapist, but she might
well find it helpful to talk to someone who was
professionally detached. I stood up and she came
to my arms to be hugged and kissed on both
cheeks, returning a kiss to one of mine.*

*Perdita took up quite a large part of my day
and I had to take some work home with me this
evening, but it was worthwhile.*

They were having a work session together the following afternoon
when Perdita started to talk about worries caused by Ingrid's
impending birthday party, and Chatwell noted that "work went out
of the window". He continued:

*She went on to talk about her misgivings in
general, and was soon close to tears. I tried to
comfort her, and several times kissed her cheeks
and forehead. She said that once she had
wondered if the best solution might be for each of
them to have another passionate relationship with
someone else, and so be able to break away from
one another.*

*Later she rang Ingrid and came to tell me that
she wasn't happy about their conversation. While
she talked I stood behind her chair and gently
massaged her neck and shoulders. When she was*

ready to leave I fetched her coat and took her in my arms for a kiss on each cheek.

It was her scalp that he massaged on the following morning, because she had a headache. And when he mentioned the possibility of a walk together at lunchtime she said she would love to do that.

> *We took a bus to Hyde Park Corner and walked to the Serpentine, where we sat for about twenty minutes in deckchairs. Then we walked round the end of the lake and spotted several birds and a couple of rabbits on the way. Caught a bus back at the Albert Hall. She seemed happy to snuggle against me in the bus, but all too soon we were back at Victoria.*
>
> *In the afternoon we worked together on plans for our first AGM. With only half-a-dozen Trustees it can be held in the office; but the most important item will be the Annual Report, which I'm going to have printed – with illustrations.*
>
> *At the end of the day she seemed quite relaxed when I helped her on with her coat, and complimented her on her appearance. Ingrid collected her in her car and I watched them go off together. Instantly animated, Ingrid was talking and gesticulating at the steering-wheel. I hope she drives carefully.*

As it happened, that was the last entry in that volume of the diary. I decided I'd had enough for one day and transferred the bookmark to the volume with the next date, in October 1984.

17

Although the sky was blue there was still a chill in the air when I walked across to Marylebone Station to buy a copy of *The Times* and take it into Valerie's Patisserie for a quick cappuccino while I scanned the headlines. I didn't linger for long because I wanted to ring Judith as soon as she got to her office, and before she started on whatever might be her task on a Monday morning. The phone was answered by the formidable Miss Hardcastle, but she was actually quite helpful, telling me that Judith had been in touch, to arrange to take a week's leave so that she could help her mother, who was recovering from an accident. I knew better than to ask for Judith's home phone number. That would have been a favour too far.

I got on with preparing the manuscript of my history of the Journalists' European Exchange Programme for presentation to the sponsors later in the week. It had turned out more or less as I had expected, unexciting but complete with all the essential facts. I wondered idly how many people might actually read it – not very many, I guessed.

At about eleven o'clock the phone rang and I was delighted to hear Judith's voice. She had rung to let me know she would be staying with her mother for the rest of the week, and she sounded pleased when I told her that I had rung her office, and that Miss Hardcastle had actually told me what had happened. Her mother was set to make a good recovery, she said, but needed to have complete rest for a few days. She hoped to return to London on Sunday evening. "I'll give you a ring when I get in," she said, to my delight.

Content that things were still going steadily in the right direction, I got to work on some picture research that my editor had asked me to do. It was finding illustrations for an article on Sir Brian Horrocks that had been submitted by the magazine's World War Two specialist. I settled down with my computer and by lunchtime had located as many pictures as were likely to be needed (subject to the absence of copyright problems, about which I would need to check with Judith next week).

Following a 'healthy' lunch of apple, Gruyere cheese and oatcakes I had a brisk walk to Regent's Park in the cool, bright sunshine. When I got back home, feeling a little virtuous, I decided to treat myself to another voyeuristic peep into the Chatwell diaries. I quickly found the volume containing my marker, and opened it at October 1984.

In the first day's entry Chatwell accompanied Perdita to buy a book by Gavin Maxwell – title not mentioned. He went on to a meeting with an NUJ official, and on his return he had tea with her.

She complained of an ache in her knees and calves. Rolled up her trouser leg and gave the calf a gentle massage, stooping several times to kiss her soft, smooth flesh, and commenting on how smooth it was. When she left I kissed her cheek and she smiled very fondly.

On the following day he took Perdita for a picnic lunch in St James's Park, where they talked "about books and butterflies". When it came on to rain he put his jacket around her shoulders and they hurried back to the office. She told him that Doctor Lang had arranged an appointment for her with a psychotherapist. Next day she rang to say she couldn't come in because she had a migraine. However, she was back at work the following morning.

She was in quite a relaxed mood, and told me she'd had a Librium. In the afternoon we had tea together and she began to talk about her 'uneasiness' with Ingrid. Soon her eyes filled with tears and I held her close, and felt her snuggling against my chest. Gradually she relaxed, and told me that Ingrid was going to visit her that evening.

The visit did not go well, and next day Chatwell wrote:

The visit from Ingrid had been marred by mutual recrimination, she said, and she talked about breaking up, but Ingrid had pleaded to be allowed 'the crumbs', and she'd decided to leave making the final break until this evening. In the afternoon Ingrid telephoned. When the call was finished she came to my room and straight into my arms. She held me very tightly, but didn't weep. For several minutes she remained in my arms and I gave her a couple of very gentle kisses. Then she began to tell me about what had happened, and we sat down side by side. When Ingrid had phoned she had braced herself and made the break. Ingrid had been angry, but not clinging or persuasive, and she had been able to remain calm.

We then got on to working on the papers for the AGM. From time to time I gave her a hug, and two or three times I kissed her cheek. And twice she proferred her cheek to be kissed.

At about 5.30 we were preparing to go home when Ingrid arrived in person! She said she had come to collect her front door keys and a book she had lent. Perdita kept very calm and went into the corridor to talk to her. I was poised to step out and interrupt if voices were raised, but it wasn't necessary. When Perdita came back into the office she was still calm, and told me what had happened. Ingrid had been angry and a bit abusive, and that had helped her to accept that the affair was really over.

I kissed her on both cheeks when she was leaving, and felt that I had got much closer to her than I had ever been before. I encouraged her to go home to her parents for the weekend, and I think she will.

The Monday diary entry said that Perdita seemed to have enjoyed her weekend, and was looking relaxed. However, he wrote that:

> *After lunchtime Perdita continued to be pleasant, but not enthusiastic in her reception of my attempts to fondle. She continued to smile, but I so much wanted a positive sign of affection and I didn't receive one.*

On the following day Chatwell wrote:

> *Perdita arrived late, saying that she'd been late in waking up. I shook my head in an admonitory way and gave her a light kiss on the cheek. No time for conversation, as I had a long meeting with Mike O'Brien from Brussels, which was very useful. Took him to lunch at Il Portico.*
>
> *After lunch she came to work with me, and told me that she'd had a letter from Ingrid – a gentle one. However, she said she had resolved to be strong. She also said she didn't think she could start again with anyone else until she'd sorted herself out. She has an appointment with the psychotherapist on Friday. When she was leaving I hugged her, and I was delighted by her yielding softness.*

"Cheerful but detached" was how Chatwell described Perdita's response to him the following morning. They had a lunchtime meeting with a journalist from Aberdeen, which he rated "successful".

After lunch she was still chatty, but seemed to be keeping her distance, very subtly evading my attempt to touch or kiss. When I laid a hand on her shoulder she swivelled her chair around; and when I tried to kiss her forehead she moved her head. I was suddenly gripped by despair.

This pattern of behaviour continued in our end of afternoon meeting. She kept her distance, while remaining cheerful. My despair grew blacker. At the appropriate time she made tea, putting a mug on my desk and taking hers back to her own office. I closed my office door in silence.

At the end of the afternoon she came back, smiling gently. She'd had a headache for the past hour, she said. I expressed concern and told her she ought to go home now. She said goodnight very naturally and I think – I hope – there may not have been anything special intended in her behaviour. Maybe it was just a temporary desire not to be touched. However, I think I'll try to raise the question again tomorrow.

I turned to the next day's entry with heightened curiosity. It began uncharacteristically with a reference to the weather – "cloudy-bright". He went on to write, "Apprehensive about today"; and I realized that he must have been writing each entry at intervals during the day, which would explain why the details were often so precise. They might sometimes have been written only minutes after the incident they described. On this morning Chatwell went on to write:

I think I will make reference to what happened yesterday and test Perdita's response. I really have very little to lose – and not much to gain, I suppose.

And I lost it all – just like that. When Perdita arrived Sumintra was with me, and so I had no opportunity to talk. However, when she joined me later to go through the papers she sat at my desk and I made coffee. I put the mugs on the desk and knelt down beside her, saying, "I'm very stupid, but yesterday I thought you were cross with me and I was so miserable." I kissed her cheek, but she moved her head away.

"I wasn't cross with you," she said, "but I wish we could just be friends without all the emotion."

I said, "You should have told me if that was what you wanted. You know I'll always do what you want." I kissed her cheek and she mumbled something incoherent, and looked unhappy.

I went back to my chair and tried to behave 'normally'. We talked briefly about TV programmes and then she took the papers to her room to cut the items we had marked. At lunchtime she went out without saying where she was going. In the afternoon I had to talk with Helen about the format for the audited accounts, and didn't see her until she was about to go home. She looked into my office to borrow a carrier bag, and said goodbye with a cheerful smile. I was not cheerful.

In the next day's entry Chatwell wrote:

Perdita phoned to say she had a bad sore throat and thought it would be better not to come in, and try to get rid of it over the weekend. She was going to try to have her psychotherapist's appointment moved to next week. I made sympathetic noises.

His entries for the rest of that day, and for Saturday and Sunday, were very brief. On the Monday Perdita was back, and Chatwell noted her voice was hoarse and so the illness must have been 'genuine'. For most of the day he was out at meetings. On the Tuesday they did the post together, and he said Perdita was talking 'normally'. She showed him a new denim jacket she had bought, and told him she'd received a tax rebate of £199. In the afternoon she offered him a satsuma, which he accepted. The following day's entry contained a surprise.

> *While we were going through the post Perdita said, "I've made it up with Ingrid. We're going to a concert together on Saturday." And she asked if she could have some time off tomorrow afternoon for her appointment with the psychotherapist – which was a formality, since she'd already arranged the appointment. Needless to say, I agreed.*

On the following day it was evident that she still wanted to have him as a confidant. He wrote:

> *When we were looking at the papers Perdita announced that she had spent the night with Ingrid, who had thrashed around a lot in her sleep, and might have been catching her cold. After lunch she went to her appointment with the psychotherapist, and although it was quite late when she got back she came to tell me about it. She had cried a lot, and thought it could have had a purging effect, releasing emotions bottled up since her childhood. I agreed, saying that I sometimes wished I could cry.*
>
> *I longed to put my arms around her, but restrained myself.*

Friday brought no significant change for Chatwell. He wrote:

> *This morning Perdita told me about problems in getting her 'pre-period' prescription from Boots. She made me a cup of tea, but otherwise made no movement towards me. I ached for her.*
>
> *She told me she was going to spend the weekend with Ingrid, and they might go to Kew. I said that even at this time of year it would probably be beautiful. As she was leaving I opened the door for her, and she seemed to jerk nervously, perhaps because she feared that I was going to touch her. Went home feeling miserable.*

As I closed the diary and prepared to fry some eggs and bacon for my evening meal I found myself sharing in Chatwell's disappointment. I wondered whether he had – perhaps unconsciously – been hoping that when Perdita broke up with Ingrid he might be able to 'catch her on the rebound'. Recalling what his nephew had told me about him losing his young wife in an accident, I assumed that there must have been a gap in his life waiting to be filled. So far I had read through only about a third of the black-covered diaries; so perhaps there was still hope for him, even though it might not be with Perdita.

18

I spent Tuesday morning in the London Library researching for an article on Prince Maurice of Orange, the champion of Dutch liberty. My research began with studies of changing tactics and weaponry and ended with reflection on the rôle of theology in the politics of the early Seventeenth Century. As I walked to Piccadilly Circus Tube station on my way home I pondered the proposition that all violent revolutionary movements with an ideological objective seemed to be doomed to tear themselves apart in conflicts between the purists, who could be content with no outcome other than perfection, and the pragmatists, who realized that compromises had to be made in order to achieve victory. The People's Front of Judea and the Judean People's Front (or their historical equivalents) really did hate each other, even more than they hated the Romans. Recalling 'The Life of Brian', I was prompted to think that Judah Maccabee might be a suitable subject for an article. He was definitely a Great Captain.

With that thought in mind I boarded a train feeling hungry and realized it was an hour past my usual lunchtime. Passing through Marylebone railway station, I bought a macaroni cheese in the Marks and Spencer food store, which meant I was able to have a hot lunch within twenty minutes. Then, feeling I had done enough work for the day, I turned again to the Chatwell diaries.

A quick flick through the pages of the volume where I had left off revealed that he had reverted to a fairly telegraphic style. On the day of JEEP's first Annual General Meeting, for example, he simply wrote: "AGM went well. Afterwards Lord Newingham gave me useful suggestion about Greece. (His father was killed there during the War)." In my second chapter I had written several hundred words on that AGM, based on the Minutes written by Chatwell.

However, Perdita's name was not entirely absent. It was evident that she still wanted to confide in him. On the Monday after his week of disappointment he wrote:

We did a paste-up sitting side by side in frustrating proximity. She looks so desirable today, in her tight-fitting jeans, with her soft hair framing that lovely face. If only her condition had been that I mustn't speak love but could continue to express it through my hands and my (unspeaking) lips I would be wildly happy.

On the Friday of that week she told him she would be spending the weekend with her American friend, Fenella. She then told him about the previous day's meeting with her psychotherapist.

She said she wasn't sure whether she wanted to be able to adjust to being a 'lover', or whether she even wanted a stable relationship. I wanted to touch as well as talk, but restrained myself. Later she was upset because she'd dropped a bottle containing the last of her favourite perfume.

On Saturday Chatwell visited Selfridges and bought an enamel container of the Guerlain scent, L'heure Bleu, "at an exorbitant price." On Monday morning he put it on her desk, with a note saying, "Please don't be angry. I wasn't looking for this but when I saw it I had to get it for you. No need to acknowledge – or reprimand me." And in the diary he commented that it would be a "reasonable final test".

Perdita came in, saw the packet and opened it, half-turning towards me with a smile. She uttered a little cry of pleasure when she saw what it was, and said, "It's exactly what I wanted." She asked where I'd found it. And that was that – no kiss, no hug. Over coffee she told me that she'd been to Kew with Ingrid on Saturday.

The following day brought an unexpected new development.

In the afternoon Perdita suddenly said she'd like to ask my advice on something. She'd been offered a job as an editorial assistant by Continental Connections, a company who publish magazines and reference books. And she had to decide by tomorrow whether or not to take it.

Trying to disguise my emotions, I asked her for details. The salary was low and the work sounded dull and routine, and she said there wasn't anything about the ambience that attracted her. We talked, and my advice was that if she wanted to get into publishing she should wait for something better. I said something about her "feeling like making a change", and she said that feeling had been stronger about a fortnight ago, when she'd applied for the job.

My deduction from all this was that she may have been asking me whether I wanted her to leave – and my answer was "no".

On the following day she told him that she'd decided not to take the job; and he said, "I'm glad you're going to be with me a little while longer." And on the day after she came back from her psychotherapy and wanted to tell him about it.

She told me there were still lots of tears. She wasn't sure if it was doing any good, but there were certainly sources of unhappiness still to be explored. In her new red sweater, with her silky luxuriant hair, she looked lovely and it was hard not to touch. Tomorrow she is having a day off, going to Oxford with Ingrid, to her friend Melanie's birthday party.

Entries in the diary over the next four weeks reverted to the telegraphic style, even though on most days there was some reference to Perdita. One day, mentioning a drug she'd been given to reduce her pre-menstrual tension, she said it seemed to have reduced her libido, but "Ingrid doesn't mind too much". About a week later she described an amusing evening she and Ingrid had had at the Lonely Well club, listening to a talk by an American woman on a new 'church' for homosexuals. In the run-up to Christmas she several times talked to him about presents she was planning to buy. A couple of days before the holiday he found a Christmas card from her on his desk. It had an unusual picture, a Japanese courtesan making a snow dog with her maids; and inside the inscription was "To Winston with love from Perdita". He gave identical boxes of Lindt chocolates to Perdita and Sumintra.

On the day when they returned to work there was a longer entry in the diary:

> When she arrived Perdita told me that she had
> broken with Ingrid on the day before Christmas
> Eve. Ingrid, she said, had been angry and
> recriminatory about not getting enough in return
> for all her attention. There were tears in her eyes,
> and I made comforting noises and touched her
> arm. Ingrid's attitude had made her angry, she
> said, and she had rejected attempts at
> reconciliation in spite of the gold pen and pencil
> set that Ingrid had insisted on giving her. I wonder
> how long this separation will last.

It didn't last long. On the following day he wrote:

> While we were looking at the few items of post
> Perdita told me that Ingrid had rung her last night
> and they were going to get back together this
> evening. Ingrid had suggested they have a talk

together in the presence of a mutual friend, an Indian woman (whom she hasn't mentioned before). She expressed scepticism about the value of professional counsellors, saying that there were other people she'd found more benefit from talking to – including me.

At the end of his entry for New Year's Eve Chatwell wrote: "And that was the end of an interesting, but very mixed, year. It felt as if I was back where I started twelve months ago."

On the first working day of the new year Perdita told him about a party she'd been to at the Lonely Well on New Year's Eve. She described it as "a bit of an orgy". There had been some smoking of pot, which she didn't approve of. And she had danced with a young woman who was an officer in the Merchant Navy, and Ingrid hadn't seemed to mind. Afterwards she hadn't felt well – a touch of food poisoning, she thought.

At the end of the afternoon on the following day Perdita came to see him in a distressed state.

She sat by my desk and wept. I made her a cup of tea and we talked. She felt that she couldn't continue with Ingrid, who was making her feel guilty, with accusations of selfishness. I said she had a right to live her life by her own standards, not by someone else's. Gradually she calmed down a little. I was tempted to embrace her, but I didn't. If she were to make a move that would be different.

Next day Perdita told him that she had finally broken with Ingrid, who had been very hostile, but she had been able to remain calm. Inevitably, two days later she reported having had a letter from Ingrid, and Chatwell warned her to expect a "campaign". About a week later she had a final session with her therapist, who had told her to accept her own sensuality and not feel guilty about it.

However, she did veer rather a lot from indulgence to abstinence. A fortnight later she reported that she was back with Ingrid.

The next few weeks occupied a comparatively small space in the diary. At the end of February Chatwell spent a week visiting contacts in Belgium, the Netherlands and West Germany, recording little more than the names of people and places. On his return to the office Perdita told him that relations with Ingrid were strained and she was thinking once more of making a break. A couple of days later she talked to him about problems (unspecified) that her friend Fenella was having in a relationship. On the following Monday morning she told him she had again broken with Ingrid. He commented:

> *It would seem that constant arrogance and nagging have finally worn her down. Tried to be reassuring, and gave her a couple of little hugs while we talked.*
>
> *In the afternoon Perdita confided that she'd just had an angry phone call from Ingrid; and she burst into tears. For a minute or so I stood with my arm around her, holding her warm body close to me, and with her hand in mine. I talked to her reassuringly, and before she left I gently kissed the side of her head.*

Next morning he noted that Perdita seemed to be in control. She had written a curt note to Ingrid, and was thinking of having a weekend away somewhere. At the end of the day he offered to walk with her through Green Park, and she accepted. She told him she was going to stay at her parents' home that night, to be away from the probable phone call. That seemed to work, because he reported that she was cheerful the next day. The day after that she left work early "because she had a headache".

On the Friday Chatwell wrote:

*At lunchtime, when we were alone, Perdita came
and showed me some photos she'd taken on her
last holiday. She stood beside me and I hugged
her waist a couple of times. Once, when she made
a teasing comment about my failure to take
photos, I patted her bottom. She laughed, and was
very friendly and confiding.*

*Very busy in early afternoon, but later Perdita
came and did a paste-up with me. Apropos of a
thunderstorm outside, I said I wished that she had
a nervous disposition, so that she would jump into
my lap for protection, and she laughed happily.
She continued friendly and affectionate, and when
she left I kissed the side of her head. I felt that at
last I was once again getting a positive response.*

With Chatwell restored to some kind of equanimity I decided I had
read enough for one day. The prospect of collecting tomorrow the
final instalment of my fee for writing the History of JEEP
prompted me to have a celebratory meal, and I phoned Giovanni
to see if he had a free table that evening. He did, and I thought
about the menu while I washed and spruced myself up for the
event. Had Judith been around to share it I would have postponed
it to the following day.

19

On Wednesday morning I went along, as arranged, to the solicitors' office, to hand over the completed manuscript of *A History of the Journalists' European Exchange Programme* to Mr. Wilfred George. He greeted me cordially, and seemed impressed that I had completed the project in good time. "I'm sure it will be a fitting memorial to Mr Bodley – and also to Mr Chatwell," he said. "I wonder how they would have viewed the current undignified exit from the EU. Do you think they might have felt that their efforts had ended in failure?"

"I'm not sure," I replied. "From what I've heard and read about them I think they were both realists. I doubt if they would have thought that JEEP could have played a significant rôle in shaping people's attitudes towards the EU. It seems to have been designed more to promote better mutual understanding among people on both sides of the Channel, and I would guess that's just as important now as it was before the decision to leave. My research, inevitably, was limited in the number of personal contacts I could make, but I did come across a number of journalists who said their attitudes had been influenced by the scheme – and most of them are now in quite influential jobs. You'll see that I've referred to that in my final chapter."

"That's good to hear," he said. "It would be a pity to think that so much effort had all been to no avail."

I assured him of my readiness to make any appropriate amendments to the text that might be thought necessary by the trustees, and he handed over the promised cheque. On my way out Miss Hardcastle told me that she'd been in touch on the previous day with Miss Mackay, and her mother was making good progress.

I banked the cheque before going home and bought a steak and kidney pie and a packet of runner beans in the station Marks and Spencer. My satisfying lunch was rounded off with a 'Pink Lady' apple. With the book still in my thoughts, it was time to continue reading the diaries.

On the Monday where my bookmark was inserted Chatwell wrote:

> *Worked with Perdita on the cuttings this afternoon.*
> *Had an irresistible desire to touch her, and I did.*
> *When she leaned across me to pick up a paper I*
> *lightly kissed her cheek. She laughed, and I put*
> *my hand on her thigh and gave a little squeeze.*
> *She told me she'd read an article in the Observer*
> *that was all about the importance for mammals of*
> *the sense of touch, and she thought it was very*
> *true. I said, "If you ever want a massage just let*
> *me know"; and she replied, "I will. I love being*
> *massaged – by the right person."*

Next day he wrote that Perdita described a new 'meditation' class that she had been to. It had included Sufidancing. She had a stiff back and he gave her a brief massage, right down to her seated buttocks. On the following day her back was still feeling stiff.

> *As she stood beside me I massaged her for several*
> *minutes, letting my hand move right down to, and*
> *over, her bottom. She purred contentedly, and said*
> *I would make a good masseur. To finish I hugged*
> *her tightly and kissed her cheek.*
>
> *Later in the day Ingrid rang her, and*
> *afterwards she came to tell me about it. The*
> *conversation had been calm, she said, and she*
> *had been willing to sympanthize, but not to*
> *concede. I congratulated her on her firmness.*

The next interesting entry was on the following Tuesday. Perdita reported on the Sufic meditation session she'd attended the previous evening, not taking it too seriously. Later in the day she came to report on another phone call from Ingrid.

*When I returned to my office I found her sobbing.
Took her in my arms and held her very close while
I talked soothingly. Ingrid had been very abusive.
Gradually she calmed down. I kissed her cheek
and she went back to work. In the afternoon she
asked if I'd like to walk with her through Green
Park on her way home. Before we left for the walk
I held her close and fondled her bottom before
kissing her cheek. At Green Park station she
thanked me for helping her to put "that bad
experience" behind her.*

The next interesting entry was on the following Monday. At the
end of the afternoon Perdita went to Chatwell's office and talked
to him about the day's events.

*Ingrid had phoned, and the conversation had been
low key. It seemed that Ingrid was beginning to be
interested in an American girl. She went on to say
that at her last appointment the psychotherapist
seemed to be upset when the subject of her
homosexuality came up. "I'm not at all sure that I
am homosexual," she said. "It's more that I'm not
comfortable with being dominated by a man." We
talked about the balance of different elements in a
relationship – intellectual, intuitive, emotional,
sensual – and she said it was the emotional that
made her afraid. I said, "You know which element
predominates in me," and she laughed and said
that she did. Kissed her on both cheeks when she
was leaving.*

The following afternoon brought an even more surprising
development in the relationship. Chatwell wrote:

At the end of the afternoon Perdita brought in a peach, which I washed for her. She gave me a bite, and I remarked that there was something else I'd be even happier to have a bit of. While we were talking I fondled the top of her thigh, clad in her 'heavenly' jeans. When she'd finished eating the peach she stood up beside me and I held her lightly round her hips, saying there was nothing that pleased me more to hold. To my delight she said that she liked being held. At that I stood up and kissed her cheeks and her neck, and fondled her bottom.

I said I was glad to hear that, because I wouldn't want to do anything that didn't give her pleasure. She repeated that she loved being held by me. I said that if there was any time when she wasn't feeling like it she must send me away. She said that of course she would, but she really did enjoy being touched by me. I stepped behind her and held her tightly, with my hands covering her breasts and my arousal pressed firmly against her pneumatic bottom, while my lips caressed her neck and her cheeks. Twice she kissed my cheeks – very lightly – and then it was time for her to leave.

It was the best day that I've had for more than a year, or more like five years, when I think about it.

Next day, as they looked through the post, Perdita told him that she'd had another letter from Ingrid, who told her she had been propositioned by an Indian woman, but had turned her down. He advised her to restrict communication with Ingrid to letters, and she agreed. They got together at teatime, and he wrote:

I put my hand on her breast for a moment and she stroked it quite tenderly. I then put my other hand on her thigh and fondled it, saying that I'd love to be able to take off all her clothes and cover her in kisses from top to toe. And I placed a few kisses on the checked shirt that covered her breast. When she stood up I kissed the seat of her jeans and then held her close from behind while I fondled her breasts through the shirt. She wasn't wearing a bra. When she had to leave she proferred her cheek to be kissed.

Intimate contacts continued on the following day. Chatwell wrote:

In the afternoon we worked on proofs together. She was suffering from pangs of indigestion and I massaged her tummy, sometimes on the bare flesh. She said she liked it because it made her feel like a baby. And she liked having her hair stroked because it reminded her of what her mother used to do to her.

Later she started talking about whether women's sexuality was different from men's. She wondered to what extent multiple orgasms were possible (which would suggest she hadn't had them – I didn't ask); and whether women experience a more ecstatic orgasm than men.

At the end of the afternoon she was still experiencing some tummy discomfort. I picked her up (she's surprisingly light) and put her over my shoulder, ostensibly to burp her, but in actuality I patted her bottom, which was conveniently placed. She giggled and seemed well pleased. When I sat her down I took her in my arms and we embraced very fondly, with kisses on her neck and cheeks

and more fondling of her beautiful bottom. Another
unexpectedly enjoyable day.

The Friday of that week proved to be yet another good day for
Chatwell.

Worked together in the morning selecting a new
batch of editors to contact. At first Perdita seemed
a little cool, and said she hadn't slept well.
However, when she yawned I cuddled her with
her head on my chest, and she said that was very
relaxing.

We talked about the pleasure of cuddling
and, emboldened, I pulled up her skirt and kissed
her naked tummy and waist, and touched her
breast. I was making her excited, she said. I told
her she'd let slip a secret – I didn't know that I
was able to excite her. Yes, I could, she affirmed.
So I took her in my arms, cuddled and fondled her,
thrusting my hand into the back of her panties to
caress her bare bottom. By now I had a strong
erection, and I hugged her from behind, pressing
against her and stroking her breasts as I kissed
her neck and cheeks. She must now be aware just
how much she excited me, I said. She laughed,
and seemed to be in no hurry to end our embraces.
I felt that our physical rapport was having some
lasting quality. With her it might fluctuate, but that
I could bear.

In the following week the pattern of Chatwell's activities,
involving a lot of meetings and interviews, left him with only brief
opportunities for being alone with Perdita. However, he faithfully
recorded every occasion when he had an intimate contact – a hug,
a kiss or a fondle. There was one report of an unsettling phone call
from Ingrid, when he consoled her with a lingering cuddle. Entries

114

for the week after became longer again. During the Monday lunch interval he had time alone with her, and he wrote:

I stood behind her chair and kissed her several times. She responded well, and so my hands began to explore. Gently I fondled her breasts, and she allowed me to go on and on. My fingers caressed her right nipple through her blouse for several minutes – it was firm but not rigid. And I thrust a hand down the back of her jeans and stroked the bare flesh of her seated bottom. Meanwhile I kissed both her cheeks, her forehead and then her ears and neck, and several times her breasts through the linen of her blouse.

When she stood up she didn't move away and I embraced her fondly, caressing her breasts with one hand and letting the other wander over her buttocks between her legs. She teased me about being like an octopus, and commented on my scratchy stubble. (I'll have to do something about that.) At one point she joked about being at the start of a materialistic stage, and said that she didn't have any morals. However, she immediately retracted, saying that she had her own morality. She tried not to hurt people; and I concurred that that was a good basic standard to set yourself. However, she said it wasn't easy, because she tended to like people who were easily hurt.

Can't remember all of our long conversation; but I know that never before has she allowed me to kiss and fondle her so warmly and so intimately. I don't know whether her desire for male caresses has reawakened and I, in the absence of anyone better, was being allowed to assuage it; but I know that I enjoyed it.

In the evening, before she left she came to my office to say goodbye. I was on the phone, but I

115

reached out a hand and drew her head close to mine, kissing her cheek and then fondling her breast. She giggled happily and blew a kiss as she went out of the door.

Opportunities for physical intimacy seem to have been fewer in the remainder of that week, although there were one or two. On the Wednesday they went out to lunch together and Perdita had a glass of wine. On returning to the office he kissed her cheek and "to my surprise she responded by kissing me on the lips, the first time she has ever done that." He returned the kiss on her mouth, but they heard Sumintra approaching the door and moved quickly apart. Later he speculated in the diary on whether the glass of wine might have contributed to "lessening her inhibitions". On Thursday Chatwell recorded one kiss and hug moment, but they had no prolonged session together. Meetings and interviews seemed to occupy most of his time. Then the late Easter Holiday intervened. JEEP closed down for ten days, including the two weekends.

Chatwell spent most of the holiday period in Florence. His diary entries reverted to the telegraphic style, but it was clear that he had visited the city before, probably several times. He had previously stayed in his chosen hotel, The Pitti Palace, and he referred to a 'favourite' restaurant, The White Boar. A comment he made about climbing up to San Miniato to survey the landscape provided a clue to his mood on the holiday. He wrote: "The magnificent view was just the same as ever but I couldn't any longer experience that sense of wonder that we used to share in days long gone."

20

I had been so absorbed in reading about Chatwell and Perdita that I didn't notice the passage of time until my stomach reminded me that it was time to eat. A can of baked beans and a couple of slices of toast, followed by a banana, provided a quick meal. Washing-up completed, and with nothing watchable on television, I decided to continue reading the diaries.

Returning from the Easter holiday on the Tuesday of the following week, Chatwell found Perdita still receptive to his caresses.

> *We came together to work in the afternoon, and I kissed her cheeks and fondled her bottom, telling her how much I had missed her. She had spent the holiday with her parents, saying that she needed to save some money for the summer. She'd had a letter from Ingrid, but it hadn't upset her. Before we separated there were a few more hugs and kisses. This evening she's going to the theatre with her friend, Fenella.*

Perdita had mentioned a book that she'd seen reviewed, on Women in Art, and on his way home Chatwell bought a copy. Next morning he put it on her desk, with a note saying, "To see something more beautiful than any of these, look in the mirror." When she came to see him, however, her first concern was to ask what she should do in response to a telephone message from Ingrid.

> *I advised her to ring back, and to keep calm. This she did, and she said that Ingrid had tried to be friendly. Then she thanked me warmly for the book. I kissed her on the mouth, but she didn't open her lips. Otherwise she was quite receptive. At the end of the afternoon she returned to my*

office and said she had a headache. She sat beside me and I massaged her neck while she talked some more about Ingrid, wanting reassurance, I think. The massage had helped a lot, she said. I cupped my other hand under her breast and fondled it gently, and she snuggled against me. When she was leaving she kissed me lightly on the lips.

Next day he noted that Sumintra was having two days' leave, to give her a long weekend holiday, and so he was looking forward to having more time alone with Perdita. He wasn't disappointed.

Shortly after her arrival I kissed and embraced her, fondling her bottom and her breasts. After we'd been through the post she began to talk about her family. It would seem that her father's withdrawn nature is a problem. And she mentioned that she had been conceived before they were married.

In the afternoon she suggested that we might do some paste-ups together, and so we sat down side by side. I made a few tentative sorties with my hands, and suddenly realized that she was actually holding up her blouse, above her left breast. Instantly I applied my lips to her nipple and discovered that it was already firm as I kissed it. I teased it with my tongue and then with my hand I began to fondle her other breast. A few minutes later I transferred my kissing and nuzzling to her right breast. All this time neither of us spoke.

Then the phone rang, with an enquiry from the printer. During the conversation I kept one hand on her breast. Afterwards she teased me

*about having sounded breathless when I was
talking.*

*I said I hoped she knew that she had only to
say 'Stop' and I would have desisted from
caressing her. She replied that she was very bad
at resisting temptation. So I think she was
enjoying it as much as I was. When we had
completed the job she stood up, and I held her
from one side and kissed her cheek, thrusting my
hand down the seat of her jeans to fondle the
exhilarating smoothness of her buttocks.*

*At the end of the day, when she was leaving,
she came to my door and blew me a kiss. I came
home feeling well contented.*

Chatwell began the following day's entry by writing, "Hoping that
I'll be able to consolidate yesterday's gains, but I know that she's
unpredictable". The morning's events seemed to justify his
caution.

*When she arrived I kissed her cheek and hugged
her. She smiled, but seemed a little reserved. I
then had to spend a couple of hours with Helen,
sorting out changes in accounting procedures,
which she had, very sensibly, recommended. At
lunchtime Perdita asked if she could spend a little
extra time, if she needed it, to find a birthday
present for her father, and I agreed.*

*Later in the afternoon we went through some
translations together. She said she had a slight
headache, which she thought was caused by
tension, not finding what she was looking for. I
offered to massage her neck and shoulders and
she accepted. After a few minutes she said that
the headache had gone, and asked, "Did someone*

teach you how to do massage?" I replied, "My wife did. She was a physiotherapist – a very good one."

Perdita looked dismayed and said, "I'm sorry, I didn't mean to... to make you think about the past."

I hugged her and said, "It's all right. I've taught myself to live in the present – most of the time, anyhow." She said she thought that was a good idea, and she also tried to do it. She then stood up to leave and I kissed her cheek. Her response was to kiss me on the lips. Encouraged by this, I inserted my hands underneath the two cotton shirts she was wearing and found her breasts. Soon I was able to pull up the shirts and kiss her nipples. Then her breathing changed – something that had never happened before – and I thrust one hand down the front of her jeans. Encountering no resistance, I unfastened the top button and eased down the zip, all the while continuing to kiss her breasts.

Now that my hand was able to go lower I felt the softness of her pubic hair. My fingers went vigorously to work, and her breathing became even faster. I glanced at her face and she seemed almost detached, but she smiled in a nervous way. With my other hand caressing one breast and my lips kissing the second nipple, we continued in a kind of rhythm for perhaps five minutes. When there was a slackening in the rhythm she indicated that she wanted to stop, and I didn't resist. I realized then that she had been stroking my back and my arms.

As I pulled up her zip she said I'd given her a lot of pleasure, and I responded by saying that made me very happy. I added that I wanted to find out all the things I could do that would give her pleasure. To that remark she didn't respond, but asked if I would like a cup of tea, and went off to make one.

When she returned I remarked that next week we were going to have to take more precautions, because Sumintra would be back in the office. She said that reminded her of something she was going to ask me. In the mornings she hated having to hurry her preparations for going out, and so she wondered if she could make a change in her working hours, starting at ten and finishing at six. And she added, "You usually work through to six, after everyone else has gone home, don't you?" Needless to say, I thought her idea was an excellent one.

As she left the office she gave me a light kiss on each cheek and said, "See you on Monday – at ten o'clock." I went home feeling elated, but reminding myself that her mood was quite capable of changing, as it had done before.

That was about the longest daily entry I had come across in the diaries. I flicked swiftly past the entries for Saturday and Sunday, which were correspondingly brief, eager to discover whether his note of caution had been justified. He wrote:

Perdita fairly subdued this morning, but proferred her cheek for a welcome kiss. When we were together with the post she talked quite a lot about the now finished (she said) relationship with Ingrid. I felt there was some physical restraint between us, but otherwise she was relaxed. Around five o'clock she complained of feeling hungry, saying it might be premenstrual tension that was giving her a craving to eat. I asked if she would like chocolate, and when she agreed I went over to Woolworth's and bought a bar of plain fruit

and nut. She was pleased, and took my kisses
and hugs as well as the chocolate.

On the following day Chatwell was out for much of the time, including a visit to the IoJ. He recorded a few quick hugs and kisses, and was "restrained because of her presumed period." Next day she told him that her period had started, and he was equally restrained. On the Thursday morning she was suffering from a hangover, having met on the previous evening a male friend called Christopher, whom she had known at Cambridge.

I held her in my arms for quite a long time, kissing
and cuddling her, while she told me about the
evening of nostalgia. Later I got her some Alka
Seltzer. At lunchtime took her to the Park, where
she lay on my jacket in the warm sun and actually
dozed off for a few minutes. On the way back I
spoke about how beautiful she had looked while
she lay asleep, and she accused me to flattery –
but I think she was secretly pleased.

Chatwell was busy with meetings on Friday morning and had no time alone with Perdita until after lunch, when she came to see him and burst into tears.

At lunchtime she had met the nurse, Dorothy, who
was a member of The Lonely Well club. Dorothy
had been briefed by Ingrid to make an
impassioned plea on her behalf. While she told me
about their conversation I sat her on my knee,
enjoying the soft pressure of her bottom on my
thigh. I calmed her down, and we talked about the
Ingrid problem. When she had accepted that she
was right to go on being firm I kissed her, and she
returned my kisses.

On the following Monday Perdita seems to have been in a more positive frame of mind. She told Chatwell about going to an art class – the first in a short course – on Saturday.

> *The teacher had told her that her first attempts suggested she had "untapped genius". Then she talked about books she was reading, including one by R D Laing. She asked me to sharpen her eyebrow pencil, and when I brought it back I stood behind her chair and gently fondled both her breasts through her red shirt. She said she was looking forward to losing sexual desire in old age. I asked if that might be because of a false guilt about sex, and she said it was more about wishing to be free and independent. The talk turned to emotional elements in relationships, which I said were often counterfeited because we thought we ought to feel strong emotions towards someone we sexually desired. She agreed, and I wished we had had more time to explore that thought.*
>
> *At the end of the afternoon, when she was leaving, I kissed her proffered cheek and briefly fondled her bottom, weighing the soft curves of her buttocks in my hands and delighting in their roundness.*

Next day he saw Perdita only briefly in the morning, but she came to his office soon after five o'clock, clearly wanting to talk.

> *The conversation got round to male chauvinism, and she said that I sometimes showed traces of it. I said that if she ever noticed me displaying a sign of it she should tell me, and I would do my best to mend my ways. I added, "I would be very happy if*

anyone thought of me as a sex object." She
replied, "It depends on who is doing the thinking,
doesn't it?"

I lent her two books on sketching that I'd
found on my shelves; and we parted with a lot of
kisses – all from me, but willingly accepted.

I had reached the final page in that volume of the diary. As I
extracted the bookmark and replaced the notebook in the box I
noted that there must be still about a dozen volumes waiting to be
read. However, I decided I'd had enough excitement for one day,
and began to prepare for bed.

21

Mindful of my need, as a freelance journalist, to keep up the search for new commissions, I set out early on Thursday morning for the London Library, to research a proposal I was going to submit to an American academic history journal, for a study of British attitudes to the Spanish-American War of 1898. When I had garnered all the information I needed I bought a cheese and tomato baguette in the Prêt a Manger in Piccadilly, and ate it on a seat in the churchyard of St James's, observing the passing scene in the sunshine.

Returned home, I got down to writing the proposal, and finished it in time to catch the postal collection in Marylebone Station. Feeling a little virtuous, I made myself a cup of tea and indulged in a further reading of the Chatwell diaries.

The next volume opened on a Wednesday. Perdita had an upset stomach and he fetched her an Alka Seltzer, and kissed her cheeks several times, noting that "she seemed to want my comfort". On the following day she admired a new, blue shirt he was wearing, saying it brought out the colour of his eyes; and he took the opportunity to fondle her breasts for a moment or two while standing behind her chair – "but not for long enough to really excite her". On the Friday she talked about her weekend plans, which included a visit to The Lonely Well club – "but I hope Ingrid won't be there". Chatwell noted, "I had hoped she might be moving out of the lesbian phase, but it seems I was mistaken."

Next Monday morning Perdita was wearing a new dress. He recorded:

It was beige cotton, clinched at the waist by a string of brown beads; scarf at her neck; brown leather boots. She looked lovely – and felt lovely, too, when I fondled her hips and bottom. She seemed pleased when I told her how beautiful she looked. Then she told me what had happened at the club on Saturday. Several girls had shown an interest in her, and Ingrid had not been there.

Later she told me the most interesting person she'd met at The Lonely Well was a lecturer in physical education at the Institute of Education, in Bloomsbury, whose name was Rosalind. They were going to meet again this evening.

When she was leaving she came to me willingly to be kissed and fondled, and said, "I'm a bit nervous about this evening. Tell you about it tomorrow."

She had a lot to tell on the following day, but they had no opportunity for private conversation until after five o'clock.

They had had dinner together (paid for by Rosalind) and had gone on to a night club, which seemed to have a gay clientele. For three hours they had danced together, and her legs were still aching, she said. After that she went home with Rosalind to her small flat in Bloomsbury. It had all been very 'cool', and it was on Perdita's suggestion that they went to bed together.

Rosalind was in her mid-forties, she said, and not specially good-looking, but very gentle and affectionate. She had been surprised by Perdita's energy, and they hadn't had much sleep. She'd enjoyed the love-making more than with any previous partner, she said.

After that she began to speculate on the future of the relationship, and was hopeful that it could be an 'open' one. Rosalind had once been married, and had a daughter who was twenty-two.

We then got on to talking about the comparative sensuality of men and women. I expressed surprise when she said she'd never been with a man who was capable of as long sustained arousal as the women she'd been with. I said I thought she'd been unlucky in her choices. The first boy she'd slept with, she said, had been mainly interested in maximising the number of climaxes he had himself. And Cedric (with whom she'd lived for a time in Cambridge) had been very considerate but still hadn't come up to feminine standards.

I said I had probably had a more limited experience, but I couldn't understand how anyone could be with her and not want to use all the time for sensual enjoyment, of which orgasm was, after all, only the climax. It was what had gone before that really mattered. Inexperienced people – which we all were initially – were often inhibited because they couldn't be sure what their partners were going to enjoy, or accept. I said I was all for 'opportunism', and for enjoying every moment of pleasure that was vouchsafed – and I tried to indicate that I would never be reluctant to accept any scraps that might be available from her table of delights.

When she finally got up to leave I took her in my arms for a hug and, to my surprise, she kissed me softly on the lips. However, when I tried to return the kiss she moved her head just a fraction, so that my kiss was on her cheek. She never fails to surprise me – talking intimately to me about her past on the day when she has started a new relationship with someone else.

On the following day he recorded that Perdita told him she had been phoned by Rosalind the previous evening. In their end-of-day encounter she complained of having cold hands, resulting from poor circulation.

I rubbed both hands and blew on her fingers, and then put one hand between my thighs to warm it while I rubbed the other. She seemed happy with this, and accepted kisses on her cheek while tentatively touching my arm.

They had a few more brief but friendly encounters on the remaining two working days of that week. On the following Monday, however, there was a new development.

When we had finished the post Perdita told me that she was starting to feel apprehensive about Rosalind's possessiveness, saying "It's like Ingrid all over again". I refrained from saying that she didn't seem very good at choosing partners, and instead took her in my arms for a cuddle. Rosalind, she said, had showed signs of wanting her to be there on hand at every available moment; and she also told some tales of jealous violence to former girlfriends.

It was clear that she wanted to get out of the relationship, and I encouraged her to act quickly and decisively, saying that otherwise she might repeat all the heartache and traumas of the Ingrid relationship. She said she thought this intensive possessiveness might be something inevitable in a lesbian affair, and it was something she didn't want. This evening she was going to phone Rosalind and tell her it was off. I hugged her tightly and several times we exchanged kisses.

On the following day Perdita didn't come to work because she had a cold. She returned on the Wednesday, saying she felt better; and she showed Chatwell an emotional, but not abusive, letter which she had received from Rosalind. He encouraged her not to weaken in her resolve to break off the relationship. And he refrained from kissing because of her cold, but hugged her tightly from behind. She stayed off work on Thursday because the cold was troubling her. Next day she returned and, to his evident dismay, told him that Rosalind had invited her to a party at the weekend, and she was thinking of accepting.

He was kept in suspense about the outcome because a return of her cold kept her out of the office on Monday and Tuesday. Although her cold hadn't completely cleared she returned to the office on Wednesday. He greeted her with kisses, but at first she was reserved.

> *After we'd gone through the post she began to talk about Rosalind, with whom she had spent a couple of days. Said she had been put off by her possessiveness and then by a lack of consideration. Already she is thinking about other possible candidates. This evening she is meeting a nurse from Barts; and even more favoured is an older girl called Trish who seems to have the correct, unclinging attitude. As she told me all this I stroked her back, kissed her hand, and once lightly fondled her breast.*
>
> *At the end of the afternoon she told me about the party at Rosalind's on Saturday. They had played the 'Truth Game', e.g. Did she want to sleep with Trish? And Dorothy, the nurse, had said she was a 'deserter', in contrast to a 'deserted'. While she was talking I put my hand down the back of her trousers and my fingertips felt the cool, soft curves at the tops of her buttocks. I took her in my arms and kissed and cuddled her before she left for home.*

On the following day Perdita told him more about Dorothy, the nurse, who, she said, was clearly very physically attracted to her. But she wasn't sure whether she wanted to let that relationship develop. She also had a dilemma about whether to meet Rosalind late at night, on her return from a holiday. Chatwell advised her against it. And they laughed together quite a lot. Next day she told him she had cancelled the Sunday night meeting with Rosalind.

She also told me about buying a pair of black corduroy trousers. I said I hoped they would fit tightly. I kissed her and fondled her bottom. Later there were two more quick kisses. I sensed that she was willing to be caressed, but not enthusiastic.

On Monday he noted that Perdita's new black corduroys were a good fit. Later in the morning she told him about her weekend.

She had been to a 'wild party', but there had been no pairing-up. Dorothy had arrived late, but wasn't so glamorous-looking. As we talked I hugged her and fondled her thigh. Gave her some grapes for her lunch.

Before going home we had another chat. She was uncertain about this evening, and feared she might drink too much and so become dependent on Rosalind. I advised her to limit her drinking to two glasses. We hugged and kissed before going downstairs.

The following morning she told him she had limited herself to two glasses and the evening had gone well.

We talked about her evening with Rosalind, and she said they had agreed to meet occasionally, on a friendly basis. She now didn't want to go to bed with Rosalind. When she was going home I gave her a satsuma.

Next day there was a Tube strike and Perdita stayed at home. On the Thursday she had a lot to talk about, and he took her to lunch at Il Portico.

She had had a phone call from Dorothy, the nurse. And she was going to have supper with Rosalind, but she didn't intend to go to bed with her – or at least she didn't think so.

She had been reading a book on 'Marital Tensions' by someone at the Tavistock, and said it had helped her to think about the influence her parents' relationship might have had on her. Maybe she was looking for some kind of amalgam of them in her sexual partners. And she wondered whether she herself really wanted to be emotional and uncontrolled, and so reacted to this trait in other people.

The lunch and conversation seemed to have given her pleasure, and back in the office she came to my arms and we kissed and cuddled intimately. I even kissed the seat of her new corduroys. When later she was preparing to go home I stood behind her and fondled her breasts, and she must have been aware of my arousal but made not attempt to move away.

Perdita reported next day on her evening with Rosalind. It had gone well, and she hadn't stayed the night. Chatwell discussed with her arrangements for the next week, when he was going to be on holiday, and they parted with hugs and kisses.

I decided that was a suitable point at which to take a break from reading and make myself a meal. There was a Waitrose salmon fillet in the fridge; and I went across to the station Marks and Spencer for a box of chips and a packet of strawberries to accompany it.

22

When I had finished the washing-up I returned to reading the Chatwell diaries. The next entries were a characteristically brief record of his holiday. He went to Switzerland to a lakeside village called Boenigen, where he had evidently been before. It provided a base from which he made daily excursions to different places in the Bernese Oberland. Some entries were as brief as: "To Thun, where I had a look at the castle and then walked to Spiez. Took the boat back to Interlaken." On a visit to Meiringen he commented: "Surprised to see a street sign saying 'Baker Street' near to the Sherlock Holmes Museum. Gave meringue another try but still found it unexciting."

On his return to London he spent a day at home but returned to the office on Friday morning. He had brought some Swiss chocolate for Sumintra, and for Perdita a tiny carved wooden bear, which delighted her.

> *When I gave her the little bear she seemed delighted, and kissed me on the lips – but only once. I kissed her cheeks several times and fondled her bottom. She showed me a new blouse she had bought – a pleasant orange colour. She had also had her hair cut and re-styled. Complimented her on it.*
>
> *There was little time to talk, with so much work to catch up on. However, we got together at the end of the afternoon and she told me that she'd had a good week – with Rosalind. She even showed me where she'd rubbed a nasty patch of skin on her elbow, the result of too energetic lovemaking in bed. One evening they had been at it for three hours, and Rosalind had marvelled at her energy.*
>
> *As we talked I fondled her thighs and kissed her several times on her cheek and neck. She*

asked about my holiday. When I mentioned going to Thun she recalled being there with her parents when they lived in Zurich, and said she would never forget looking out on a bright, summer morning across the lake to the Jungfrau.

She said that tomorrow she is going to a concert with Rosalind. As we parted I kissed her again, hungrily, and she gave me a kiss on the cheek.

On the following Monday, while they were going through the newspapers and magazines she drew his attention to an article about bottoms.

The writer said that the most important characteristic of a bottom was that it should be friendly. Saying that I strongly agreed, I tipped her sideways on her chair and fondled, patted and kissed her corduroy-clad buttocks while she giggled. She began to talk about her own sexuality, saying it seemed to go in waves – and was on a high just now. Rosalind told her she'd never met anyone so sexually active. I put my hand down into the seat of her trousers and was allowed to leave it there, fondling the delicious softness of her naked flesh.

She told me that during the weekend there had been a dinner party at Rosalind's, and a lunch with a married friend. Rosalind had tried to persuade her to move in, but she had resisted. She needed to maintain an area of independence, she said, and wasn't happy thinking about any kind of 'marriage' arrangement.

We left the building together at the end of the afternoon and Rosalind was waiting outside in a car. I caught just a glimpse of her – a refined

134

*masculinity about her face, combined with a
certain matronliness. She's my age!*

Next day Chatwell joked with Perdita about the fact that he was
the same age as Rosalind. While they were talking he laid his hand
on her breast and she stroked it several times.

> *She said she was a bit apprehensive because
> Rosalind had been talking about buying a farm
> and going to live on it together. She wasn't sure if
> it had been meant seriously. When she joked
> about slimming it gave me the opportunity to urge
> her not to, while I fondled her bottom and her
> breasts, pretending to 'count her ribs'.*

On Wednesday he visited the dentist in the morning and had only
a brief time with Perdita in the afternoon. On Thursday he took her
to lunch at Il Portico. They had an animated conversation, and he
wrote:

> *We talked about having 'controlled' personalities,
> and about how we both felt an urge to be more
> irresponsible and childish as we grew older. She
> thinks that in puberty she might have generated
> 'psycho-kinetic energy' – possibly with sexuality
> as its origin. It was a warm, intimate time which
> we were both reluctant to bring to an end.*
>
> *Later in the afternoon we worked together
> and I hugged her closely as we talked, and kissed
> her passionately on the neck. My hand found its
> way into the back of her jeans and I caressed the
> cool, smooth flesh of her flank. For a joyous
> moment she put a hand on my thigh and stroked it
> tentatively.*

On Friday Perdita confided that she was suffering from cystitis, and thought it might have been caused by sexual hyper-activity with Rosalind on Monday.

I tried to be comforting and sympathetic, but there was not much I could do. She came to me for kisses and a cuddle. This evening she is going to be with Rosalind, and I advised her to exercise restraint, and also suggested she see a doctor if the pain didn't go away.

After the weekend Perdita did see a doctor, on Monday morning, making her late for work. She'd been given a prescription and was beginning to feel more relaxed. Chatwell wrote:

When we got together in the afternoon she started talking about the absurdity of thinking that lovemaking should only happen at night. I agreed, and said why should people who had opportunity during the day postpone it until bedtime? She certainly didn't, she said. Then she remarked that the doctor had tested her and found no infection. It must have been caused by too vigorous lovemaking. I cuddled her tightly and kissed her cheek.

She said Rosalind had suggested they go to Paris on holiday together, towards the end of the month. She liked the idea because there was so much she wanted to see in Paris, where she'd been only once, with her parents. She thought Rosalind's interest in Paris was more that she saw it as a glamorous place in which to be with a lover.

I said that if they decided to go I'd be happy to lend her my Blue Guide, adding, "We spent some very interesting times there." And I warned that if they went in July or August they would need to keep themselves well hydrated – with non-alcoholic drinks. "It's the time when all the Parisians go off to the seaside, or the mountains." She thanked me, and hoped they could decide the date soon, so that she could book it.

During the rest of that week Chatwell recorded a few kisses and hugs every day but no significant conversations. In the following week, when the weather was hot, he had a walk one day with Perdita in St James's Park. They sat on the grass, and she talked about Rosalind being a little bit prudish – she'd been reluctant to take a bath together.

I said it was no wonder she didn't want to display herself alongside Perdita's beautiful body. She said she thought it was her sensuality that attracted Rosalind most of all. We then got on to age differences, and she said she didn't think of me as being older – and I confirmed that I didn't think of her as younger. Sometimes she liked the idea of reverting to childhood, she said.

On the Friday Perdita was wearing a dress – because she had already packed other clothes in preparation for the holiday, she said.

At the end of the afternoon I had an opportunity to explore. She wasn't wearing a slip, and the softness of her hips and her buttocks beneath my hands was unbelievable. I commented on how deliciously soft she was, and she laughed delightedly, saying that she actually felt naked, with no bra or slip and only a brief pair of panties. I knelt behind her, pulled up her skirt and began to kiss her thighs and pantied bottom (paper, disposable panties, I think). I had intended to be

137

*restrained (comparatively) but the beauty of her
nether regions overcame me, and I pulled down
the waistband of the white panties and kissed her
bare bottom, my lips caressing the cleft between
her buttocks, which seemed as soft and yielding
as her lips. Then, with a great exercise of
willpower, I pulled up the panties and allowed her
skirt to drop. I took her in my arms, kissed her
cheeks and briefly fondled her breasts. I was
allowed to carry her suitcase to the station. (She's
spending the night with Rosalind, before they
begin their journey tomorrow). Gave her a parting
kiss.*

Now I won't see her for a fortnight.

Over the next fortnight the diary entries were minimal. Then, on
the Friday of the second week Perdita returned after her holiday.
Chatwell wrote:

*She looked well, and was sun-tanned, with a few
freckles. As I was with Sumintra when she arrived
there was no opportunity for a kiss until we got
together later to go through accumulated cuttings.
Then she came very willingly to be embraced, and
said the holiday had gone reasonably well. They
had visited most of the places in which she was
interested – the Louvre, Malmaison, Fontainbleau,
Monet's garden, Rodin's house, Les Deux Magots
for coffee (on my recommendation). She had
bought a pair of pyjamas as a 'thank you' gift for
Rosalind.*

*Had some more chat about Paris at the end of
the afternoon; and she came to me to be kissed on
both cheeks. Helped her carry parcels to the
station; and as commuters scurried past on either
side she put up her cheek to be kissed.*

On Monday Chatwell was busy with meetings for most of the day, but at the end of the afternoon he got together with Perdita, and noted that when he kissed her cheek she came to him "quite willingly, several times". Later she began to talk about her relationship.

She told me she was trying to discreetly persuade Rosalind to slim. I said that she herself had no need to slim, and I fondled her small, firm breast as I talked. My hand was allowed to linger on its softness, covered only by her shirt, for more than a minute. She went on to talk about personal habits of Rosalind's that upset her, e.g. using her pyjamas and leaving a stain (from her period) on them.

When I kissed her lightly on the cheek she put her arms around me and hugged me. She said she wanted to spend a bit more time on her own, so that she could develop her interests. Encouraged her to follow that course.

Two days later he wrote that Perdita told him she had been thinking of leaving Rosalind, but decided to stay with her until after they'd had a September holiday together. After receiving that news he noted that he had "raised her blouse and kissed her naked waist, ticking her belly-button with my tongue. She seemed to enjoy it." There were two more similar episodes in the next two days of the week.

Chatwell went on holiday in the following week, to Bologna, which he used as a base to explore nearby places, including Ravenna, which seemed to hold treasured memories for him. But, as always with his records of holidays, the diary entries were minimal.

I decided to have an early night, and closed the black-covered notebook and replaced it in the box.

23

On Friday morning my editor phoned while I was finishing breakfast and asked me to research illustrations for an article on Shaka and his conquests in southern Africa. Accordingly, I spent the morning at the London Library, and by lunchtime had found what I needed. I returned home somewhat shell-shocked by the endless accounts of slaughter and calculated cruelty perpetrated by that military genius. Oddly enough, it reminded me of the research I had done a year earlier on Mao Zedong.

I had just finished the lunch washing-up when the telephone rang. It was my parents, ringing because I had forgotten to make my customary weekly call to them on Thursday evening. As usual, my mother wanted to be reassured that I was having enough to eat. My father asked what I made of the news that Theresa May had failed to reach agreement with Labour Party leaders, and so was unlikely to have a majority in the Commons for her Brexit deal. I hadn't given the news much thought, but agreed that there seemed to be just a remote possibility that Brexit might not happen after all. He said that one of his Dutch colleagues had commented that British politics were beginning to look more like the Continental variety, just as we were about to leave Europe.

After a quick call to my editor to bring him up-to-date on what I was planning for the Shaka article illustrations I was in the mood to return to the Chatwell diaries. On his first day back from his Italian holiday he gave Sumintra a box of 'Baci di Dama' biscuits (which I guess translates as 'Ladies' Kisses'). For Perdita he had a lavishly illustrated book on the mosaics of Ravenna. When they were alone together he presented it to her, and she was evidently delighted with it, and kissed him on both cheeks.

She had had her hair cut, and accepted my comment that I preferred it longer, even though the new style had its attractions.

We got together again at the end of the day.
She said she was beginning to feel a bit
'claustrophobic' with Rosalind, who has become
more physically clinging. She's worried about the
relationship, but said she wanted to avoid being
'hurtful'. I hugged her and slipped my hand down
the waist of her jeans to touch the top of her
buttocks. When she was leaving she thanked me
again for the book and we exchanged kisses.

On the following day Perdita talked about the possibility of a holiday in September with Rosalind, and she said she'd like to go somewhere that had butterflies to watch. She'd heard that Norfolk was good for some species. During the rest of that week he had several more affectionate encounters with her, but no interesting conversations. In the next week she was busy making preparations for a holiday in Southwold, and several times asked for his advice.

While she was away the diary entries once again became telegraphic, and it was not until Tuesday, 11th September, that he resumed making a more detailed record. He wrote.

To work early. Went through the post with
Sumintra, but there was little of interest. Suddenly
Perdita was back, coming into my office to greet
me. Since we were not alone I didn't kiss her, but
an hour later I went to her office and made up for
lost time. She was in a receptive mood, and as
well as accepting my kisses and hugs she allowed
me to fondle her bottom and kiss her breasts
through her thin cotton shirt. I felt her nipples
stiffen under my lips and was encouraged to
continue. Quickly undoing a couple of buttons I
slipped my hand inside the shirt and gently
touched each lovely little breast. She allowed my
fingers to remain in contact for a couple of minutes
before gently removing my hand. I kissed her
lightly on the lips.

*Then she began to talk about the holiday,
which had not been an unqualified success.
Among Rosalind's faults had been unpunctuality,
which had made them miss a concert they were
planning to attend. She had seen a few beautiful
butterflies, including a Humming-bird Hawk Moth,
but not as many as she had hoped for, because
Rosalind had wanted to spend a lot of time by the
seaside. She remarked, "I think I might even be
beginning to prefer men" – which greatly
encouraged me.*

*Saw her again at the end of the afternoon,
when she complained about feeling tired – she
hadn't yet had a chance to recover from the
holiday. We kissed on the lips before leaving for
home.*

Next day Chatwell asked Perdita to draft an appendix for their
forthcoming Annual Report. It was to be a compilation of extracts
from articles in Continental publications involved in the
programme. He wrote:

*I think it's time to give her something that will
stretch her intellectually. She seemed pleased at
the prospect.*

*At lunchtime I bought her a copy of the new
translation of a Colette novel that I'd seen
reviewed in the Times. Left it on her desk with a
note saying, 'Something to read in the sunshine'.
When she came in to thank me she said, "You
must be telepathic. I've been thinking that I
wanted to read a Colette".*

*Before she left I kissed her cheeks and
fondled her bottom through her light, summer
trousers. When I said that her contours excited me*

even more than the Alps she pretended to
disbelieve me but was, I think, secretly pleased.

On Thursday morning Perdita phoned to say she would be late in because she had an appointment with her doctor. When she arrived, just before lunchtime, she told Chatwell that the doctor had diagnosed bladder spasms, possibly caused by tension. He wrote:

> *She said she was feeling better now that the*
> *cause of her discomfort had been identified. Later*
> *in the afternoon we worked together and she*
> *seemed to be very relaxed. She was wearing her*
> *flimsy black dress and the temptation was*
> *irresistible. I fondled her bottom through the thin*
> *cotton and then knelt behind her and kissed it.*
> *Stroking her bare thighs underneath her skirt, I*
> *stood up and held her by her hips while I kissed*
> *her cheeks for several minutes. When I asked if*
> *she would wear the "seductive dress" again*
> *tomorrow she said that she might; and she blew*
> *me a kiss when she was leaving.*

She did wear the dress again on the following day, and he commented:

> *I did just once penetrate the fold to place my hand*
> *on her naked thigh, but I wasn't allowed to remain*
> *for long. However, I hugged her and kissed her*
> *brown arm and her cheek. At lunchtime she came*
> *with me to the Capri, a pleasant little place which*
> *Basil had discovered across Eccleston Bridge. She*
> *talked about how her therapist had told her that*
> *she had "a confident lack of confidence". And once*
> *again she is thinking about whether she ought to*
> *leave Rosalind.*

143

At the end of the afternoon, while I was standing behind her chair, I put both hands on her breasts. Twice she gently removed them, but the third time she allowed them to remain while I fondled very gently. I felt her nipples rise and grown firm beneath my fingers, and I kissed her cheek and neck. She stood up and I pressed myself – very aroused – against her bottom and hugged her tightly, kissing her passionately, sometimes at the side of her mouth, and also on her breasts. Several times she stroked my arms and my shoulders, but eventually she gently pushed me away. Neither of us said anything about what we had been doing as we prepared to go home.

After a weekend spent with Rosalind Perdita was thinking seriously about making a break.

She talked intimately about her problems with Rosalind, while I was allowed to stroke her back and, briefly, to fondle her breasts. She even seemed to want my kisses on her cheek. Then she said she'd had an erotic dream about me last night, but refused to tell me what it was.

As she was leaving I said, "I hope I'll have an erotic dream about you tonight," and she laughed and blew me a kiss from the doorway.

On the Wednesday Perdita had completed the draft for the Annual Report and Chatwell was pleased with it. (I remembered using several extracts from it in one of my early chapters.) He had only brief encounters with her on the following two days. The weekend was a decisive time for Perdita. In Monday's entry Chatwell recorded:

144

Perdita told me that she had broken with Rosalind on Saturday. She said she was looking forward to having a lot more time on her own to do the things that really interested her. She came to me to be kissed on her cheeks and her neck, many, many times. I stroked her bare back underneath her sweater, and twice I touched her bare breasts, but the nipples weren't erect.

At lunchtime I took her to the Capri and she talked about improvements she wants to make in the furnishings of her rented flat, now that she would be spending a lot more time there. Jungian symbolism was another subject that interested her. I squeezed her knee a few times under the table, and she seemed pleased.

On the following day Chatwell bought a hand-held electric beater on his way to work, and presented it to Perdita as an encouragement to spend more time in her own kitchen. He was rewarded with kisses, and took the opportunity to fondle. Chatwell began Wednesday's entry:

Another mellow autumn day. Had hoped for a walk at lunchtime, but there wasn't time. In late afternoon Perdita came to my office and I stood up to kiss her cheek. She was wearing her new grey-green jeans, which hug the cleft of her bottom very closely, and I couldn't resist the impulse to fondle. I moved behind her and pressed my excitement against her bottom while I fondled her breasts through her soft woollen sweater. I felt her nipples rising as I kissed the back of her neck. My body began involuntarily to simulate the movements of coitus and I could feel her responding. She turned around and we continued our embraces face to face.

Very daring, I gently kissed her mouth. She didn't resist and I repeated the kiss, feeling her lips responding to mine. For maybe two minutes we kissed passionately, mouth to mouth, our bodies straining against each other and my hand caressing her softness. I whispered how beautiful she was, and saw that she smiled shyly in response. "You're very dear to me," I whispered, and went on to say that I would love to kiss her all over, starting at the top of her head and ending at the soles of her feet.

I added that she needn't be afraid I would do anything she didn't want me to do. Then, thinking she had demurred, I asked her if she didn't trust me.

"It's more that I wouldn't trust myself," she replied. I said that she could always set the limits and be sure that I would keep within them. Then she said, quite reluctantly, I thought, that it was time for her to leave. We kissed again on the lips, and she accepted my offer to carry her bag to the station. There she came to me for a kiss on her cheek, saying affectionately, "See you tomorrow".

On the next day, however, she phoned to say that she had a cold and wouldn't be coming in. On Friday the cold was still troubling her, and Chatwell's diary entry was only six lines long.

24

I closed the diary and decided it was time to have dinner. It would be a good idea, I had earlier resolved, to demonstrate my culinary skill to Judith on the first occasion when she came home with me to have a meal. With any luck that might be going to happen in the coming week, and so it was time to practise what I was going to cook for her. Wiener Schnitzel was the main course, something with a hint of sophistication but not too complicated to cook. I was well satisfied with the result, and as I did the washing up my thoughts were straying to what I hoped might be Judith's reactions after she had eaten. And that prompted me to wonder how Chatwell might have handled the situation – and so I returned to reading the diaries.

The bookmark had been inserted at the end of a week. On the following Monday, which was October 1st, Perdita had returned to work, having recovered from her cold. It was a day when Chatwell had several meetings, but she went to see him on arrival, and when he hugged her tightly she told him, "You're nice and warm", and rewarded him with a kiss. The next three days were busy with preparations for the forthcoming annual general meeting, but on each he managed to have a short, intimate session with her.

When the annual general meeting arrived (I remembered reading the very full minutes) it received only a brief mention – "Went very well". However, Chatwell also noted that Mr Bodley had afterwards taken his niece, Perdita, to lunch at the Connaught.

When she returned late in the afternoon she told me that Bodley appeared to be well pleased with the way in which things are going in JEEP. But their conversation had been mainly about family affairs, with which he was out of touch, and wanted to bring himself up to date. Perdita is worried about lumps in her groin, and has an appointment with the doctor tomorrow. I kissed and cuddled her before she left for home.

When she arrived, just before lunchtime on the following day, Perdita told him that the doctor had been reassuring, and there was nothing to worry about.

Asked her if she had bought a TV licence for the flat, and when she said 'no' I offered to pay for it, saying she could repay part when her finances had recovered. She took up the offer and bought it at lunchtime.

At the end of the afternoon I was allowed to fondle and kiss her breasts (through her sweater) and to fondle her bottom quite intimately. She kissed me on the cheek when she was leaving.

Reading the following Monday's entry I was as surprised as I think Chatwell must have been by the turn of events. He wrote:

Perdita seemed excited when she arrived at the office this morning. When she came in to do the post she announced, "I've met a man who likes me." On Saturday she had gone to Reading with her American friend, Fenella, to visit a mutual friend from college days called Samantha who was working there as a teacher in a girls' school. Samantha had had an invitation to a dance at the University of Reading and had taken them both along with her ("they want as many women as they can get"). There she had encountered a post-graduate student who, at the end of the evening, had invited her to spend the weekend with him – when his flatmate was going to be away.

"His name is Oliver Granville," she said, "and he comes from Ireland but he doesn't sound at all Irish – more like a 1950s BBC newsreader. I

asked him about it and he quoted the Duke of Wellington – something about a man who's born in a stable not being a horse."

I said he must be from the old Anglo-Irish aristocracy. I'd met a couple of them. One, who did work for the BBC, as it happens, had an accent that made the Queen sound middle-class. She laughed and said that was exactly right. He'd told her that one of his ancestors had gone to Ireland with Strongbow. She said she hadn't wanted to sound ignorant and so she hadn't asked him to explain what that meant. I told her briefly what I knew about the twelfth century Earl of Pembroke and the Anglo-Norman conquest of Leinster. "That makes sense," she said. "It's like people who brag that they had an ancestor who came over with William the Conqueror".

He had danced with her all evening, she said, making the suggestion about going for the weekend when she was leaving. He was very good looking, she added; but she thought he probably wasn't very intelligent. He was a doing a short course at Reading to help him with running the family farm, which one day he'd be taking over from his father.

Because she'd arranged to go to a concert at the Festival Hall that evening with Fenella I invited her to have a meal with me first at the Capri. She had salad and a glass of wine and I had an omelette. We talked a little about her decision to have a 'new adventure'; and I reminded her that if she was going to stay the night with this young man she would need to think about contraception. She agreed, and said she would ring Doctor Lang tomorrow, to see if he would fit her with a 'cap'.

Went home feeling disappointed, but not despairing.

149

In the next day's entry Chatwell recorded that Perdita was more subdued, and seemed a little uncertain about her decision. She had rung Doctor Lang, however and arranged an appointment for Friday morning. On Wednesday several meetings prevented him from having more than a brief encounter with her. And on Thursday he walked with her to the station at the end of the afternoon, when "as usual" she proferred her cheek for a farewell kiss. On Friday he wrote:

She came to see me when she returned from her appointment with Doctor Lang. For some reason he hadn't been able to fit the cap today, but he had given her a packet of condoms. I kissed her cheeks and fondled her bottom.

At lunchtime she came with me to the Capri. We had a long and fairly intimate chat. She talked about her childhood, her mother's affairs, her father's disillusionment and depression, and about the need to be optimistic. Enjoyed her company.

When she was leaving at the end of the afternoon I held her close to me for some time, kissing her cheeks and fondling her bottom. I warned her to be very careful and sent her off with an admonitory pat on the seat of her 'tapestry' dress.

I turned with renewed interest to the entry for the following Monday. It was surprisingly short, but to the point.

She came and told me about it. They had gone to bed together. (She'd made him use a condom.) She said she'd enjoyed it, but wasn't ecstatic, and indeed seemed to have some doubts about

*whether she wants to continue the relationship.
Oliver's only previous experience of sex might have
been with a prostitute, she suspected.*

*In the afternoon before the intimacy, she went
on to say, they'd gone for a walk in the
countryside and he had suddenly kissed her. It
had given her such a feeling of relief that she had
burst into tears. Of course she couldn't tell him the
real reason why she was crying, and made up
something about "release of tension after a
difficult week." I refrained from asking why she'd
never burst into tears on any of the occasions
when I had kissed her over the past months –
maybe because I didn't want to hear the answer.*

*Before she left she came willingly to my arms
and I kissed her cheeks and fondled her bottom.*

On the following day Chatwell recorded a long conversation,
saying:

*Perdita seems a bit depressed and uncertain
about the future. I encouraged her to think that
she could use her freedom creatively, and not be
afraid of loneliness. For a while she sat on my
knee, and liked it when I put my hand under her
sweater and stroked up and down her naked
spine.*

*She said she was going to book another
session with her psychotherapist, because she felt
a need to sort out her fear of making any lasting
relationship. And her attitude to men was still
ambivalent. She wanted to reject anyone who
mirrored her father, and yet she wanted a
relationship with someone who would take care of
her.*

151

Later, when we walked to the Tube together,
she held up her cheek for a farewell kiss.

Perdita was still in a talkative mood on Wednesday. Chatwell wrote:

> *She came into my room first thing this morning.*
> *Today she's having her period, and so I was*
> *restrained in my caresses, but raised her sweater*
> *a couple of times to kiss and stroke her bare back.*
> *She talked of her doubts about Oliver, and also*
> *about her fear of the side-effects of various kinds*
> *of contraception.*
>
> *To my surprise, she told me she was going to*
> *have lunch with an accountant she had met on the*
> *train from Reading. At the end of the afternoon she*
> *told me how the lunch had gone, saying that he*
> *had seemed keen but she was not. He had been*
> *divorced, has two children and is forty-two. He*
> *gave her roses and wants to see her again, but*
> *she is not sure. She allowed me to hug her and*
> *kiss her cheeks as we talked. I told her she didn't*
> *have to hurry her decisions because there would*
> *be no shortage of men desiring her company.*
> *Before she left I kissed her again and fondled her*
> *bottom. In spite of her roving mood she does seem*
> *much closer to me now.*

On Thursday afternoon Perdita informed him that Oliver had rung her and she had told him she didn't want to continue the relationship, even though she had felt somewhat reluctant to end it. On Friday, however, she had changed her mind.

> *She said she had found his phone number and*
> *had given him a ring. Needless to say, he had*

*invited her to visit him tomorrow. She allowed me
to caress her as we talked, even permitting a few
exploratory touches of her breast through her
sweater. It was delectably soft to my fingers. At
one point she said, "I keep thinking about things
I'd like to do tomorrow night." She hoped he
wouldn't be put off because it might be the end of
her period. I said he'd be an idiot if he was. But I
felt disheartened.*

*At the end of the afternoon she told me she'd
had a call from Rosalind, who had been amiable
and seemed to be making new friends. Then she
mentioned that she was "half-regretting" her
decision to drop the accountant. We laughed
together over her desire to have a second string to
her bow.*

Perdita was very forthcoming about the weekend when they got
together on Monday morning. Chatwell wrote:

*She was full of chat about the success of the
weekend, and went on to describe in detail how
her newly-fitted 'cap' had been uncomfortable,
and how Oliver had said it had hurt his penis. I
advised her to have another talk with the doctor.
As we talked she allowed me to kiss her cheek
and neck and even to leave my hand on her breast
(through her 'tapestry' dress) for several minutes.*

*Oliver has invited her to visit his home in
Ireland during the Christmas holiday period,
possibly around the New Year. I encouraged her to
accept – secretly thinking that the experience
might end the relationship. Later, she said she'd
found out that his first experience of sex had been
with a prostitute, as she'd suspected. He'd also
told her that his former girlfriends had both been –*

and remained – virgins. He'd responded to her with great enthusiasm, but she thought he seemed insecure.

Had just a quick kiss and cuddle with her at the end of the afternoon.

Throughout the rest of November diary entries were fairly brief, with no more startling revelations, although Chatwell continued to record more kisses and embraces, some of them quite intimate. Early in December Perdita again visited Oliver in Reading and reported that it had been "all right". They had planned the timing of her visit to Ireland at the end of the month.

Chatwell spent his New Year holiday in Milan, staying at the Hotel Leonardo da Vinci, and arranging to arrive on January 2nd, so that the numerous galleries he wanted to visit had reopened. Included, of course, was a visit to Leonardo's 'Last Supper'.

Deciding to postpone until tomorrow finding out what happened when Perdita visited Ireland, I closed the diary and began to prepare for bed.

25

On a dull Saturday morning which gradually brightened up I walked to Waitrose in Marylebone High Street and did my weekly shopping. Returned home, I did some cleaning and polishing in the flat, inspired by the thought that some time in the coming week I might be entertaining Judith. In the hope that it might be one of the earlier days of the week I even bought some late daffodils from the Marylebone Station Marks and Spencer's. It was then time to have some haddock fishcakes and oven-ready chips for lunch; and when I had finished the washing-up I returned to reading the Chatwell diaries.

On the Monday morning after the Christmas holiday Chatwell was busy, but he invited Perdita to join him for lunch at Il Portico, no doubt as interested as I was to learn what had happened on her visit to Ireland. He wrote:

She began to tell me about the trip as we walked to Il Portico. Oliver had met her in Dublin Airport and taken her home in the family car – a station wagon, she thought it was called. There she was greeted by his parents and his younger sister, Maud. They lived in a big, rambling country house that was "more than a farmhouse but less than a manor". Needless to say, she was assigned a bedroom of her own, next to Maud's.

Next day she met various family members and friends, who were "quite hospitable". They all went clay pigeon shooting, which was "incredibly boring, but better than shooting live birds". She had declined to take part, not wishing to hurt her shoulder with the recoil of the gun. "At this time of year there weren't even any butterflies to look for," she said.

In the course of the day she had heard quite a lot about the family. Oliver's father had a cousin who was a viscount – an Irish one; but he had gone to live in Canada. "I got the feeling they thought I would be impressed," she said.

After prep school Oliver had gone to a public school across the Border in Northern Ireland, called Portora Royal. Its most famous alumnus was Oscar Wilde, of whom Oliver had remarked, "I suppose he was a great writer, but his disgusting behaviour was something decent people didn't talk about."

Perdita said, "The best part of the trip was the ride back to Dublin Airport. I think I should try to let Oliver down gently. Maybe I'll have a bad cold. As a reason for not seeing him I could spin that out for a fortnight; but then I'll have to tell him it's not on."

On the way back to the office she told me she'd heard that Rosalind had a new girlfriend, a 20-year-old. Said that made her feel happier about having "abandoned her".

She came to see me again at the end of the afternoon. As we stood together I put my hand up the skirt of her linen dress and fondled her bottom for several minutes. She also allowed me to stroke her naked thigh, and I kissed her left breast through her dress. When she was leaving she kissed me very lightly on my lips. Taken by surprise, I returned the kiss, equally lightly.

On the following day Perdita worked with him in her office on some translations. Having seen a report somewhere of the film "The Women's Room", she began talking about the disadvantages of marriage. She also told him she was going to visit her parents next weekend. Then she surprised him by saying she was thinking about the possibility of looking for another girlfriend, instead of a man. He wrote:

She went on talking, and I urged her to think of some positive things to do, so that her life became more her own. We'd spent a lot of time talking, I said, but she should know that I'd now be able to work twice as hard because of the time I'd spent with her. Then I kissed her tenderly on both cheeks and went back to my own office.

On the following day they got together in the afternoon. Chatwell wrote:

She said she'd had a call from Gerald, the divorced accountant she'd met on the train, who apparently hasn't give up trying, and she'd agreed to meet him. She was in one of her "sensation-seeking moods," she said.

While we talked my hand had been fondling her stockinged thigh beneath her red corduroy skirt. I moved it up and began to caress her mons veneris – through panties, of course. She allowed me to continue for a few minutes before removing my hand. I kissed her thigh, and when she stood up I raised her skirt at the back and kissed her bottom through her white panties. Then I stood up and hugged her tightly from behind, saying "It was a great privilege to be allowed to kiss the most beautiful bottom in London."

She laughed and said, "You can't possibly know that. You haven't seen all of them." And I replied, "I know that nothing can be better than perfection, and perfection is how I would describe this pulchritudinous posterior" – fondling it and delighting in its pneumatic softness under my fingers. She laughed again and said, "Well, at least it compensates for the smallness of my breasts. I used to worry about that when I was at school."

Transferring my fingers to her angora-sweatered breasts, I said, "In my opinion these are perfect, too. Much better than barmaids' balconies, that only get in the way when you're having fun. I hope one day you'll let me show you just how much pleasure these little beauties can give to you, and to me, when they're not covered up. And, of course, you don't have to waste money on bras." She laughingly conceded that it was an advantage, while gently removing my fingers from her breasts.

She then turned round, but didn't move away, and actually stroked my back, a few times while I kissed her cheeks. At that point I had to take a phone call, and the mood was lost. Walked with her to the Tube and kissed her cheek when she left.

Thursday was a busy day and Chatwell recorded only one brief contact with Perdita. She told him that Gerald had phoned again, and she was going to be seeing him at the weekend. He wrote: "One step forward, two steps back." On Friday Perdita asked if she could have lunch with him and he took her to the Capri.

She talked about the problems of living in a family, and in particular about her horror of big family weddings. And then she mentioned that she had been thinking about using a marriage bureau. Said she doesn't much care for theatre, preferring cinema. When she wondered if she might get involved in writing something I strongly encouraged her. Then she talked about a book on marriage by a Jungian, which said that women needed to have a variety of 'models' from which

*they could select one to copy. Sounded like an odd
idea.*

*When we got back to the office she thanked
me, and kissed me on both cheeks.*

The following Monday inevitably had a report from Perdita on
what had happened in her encounter with Gerald, the divorced
accountant.

*Snatched a few minutes with Perdita between
meetings. She said that Gerald had been "good
fun" in bed, but she wasn't sure that he was right
for her. He'd told her that he wasn't much good at
passing exams; and his relationship with his
children seemed pretty confused.*

*Saw her again at the end of the afternoon.
She'd been at lunchtime to look at some sweaters
in the sales but hadn't liked them. Kissed and
cuddled her while we talked, and when she stood
up I fondled her bottom through her silky-textured
red trousers. When I kissed her breast through her
angora sweater I got a strand of wool on my lips,
much to her amusement. Walked with her to the
Tube.*

For about the next six weeks the diary entries followed the same
pattern. On most days Chatwell had some time with Perdita, and
usually there were kisses and caresses. She quickly abandoned the
relationship with Gerald and then, to his surprise she registered her
interest with the Heather Jenner Marriage Bureau. Thereafter she
reported at least one meeting with a potential suitor every week,
but none of them ever reached the bedroom. Her reports were
usually quite brief – or it may have been that Chatwell didn't
choose to record them in detail. Of the half-dozen hopefuls three
were divorcees and two were widowers; and all were significantly

older than Perdita. Then, one Monday morning in March Chatwell wrote:

Perdita came to see me and appeared to be depressed. She said she was fed up with talking to men who only seemed to be eager to unload their problems on to her. She'd decided to stop using the marriage bureau. I cuddled and kissed her, and eventually she shed a few tears. But talking seemed to cheer her up; and when she noticed that her sweater had shed some hair on to my jacket she went to her office to fetch a brush that would get it off. When she returned we stood side by side, and I fondled her bottom through her green corduroy skirt as we talked. She was responsive and I became very excited. My hand went up under her skirt and my fingers found their way under the elastic of her panties, so that they were able to touch the delectable softness of her buttock. She just continued to talk.

Why was it that some people had more sensuality than others, she wondered. I said there could be no doubt about the generous amount that she had, and I thought that I could probably match it.

She was going to meet her American friend, Fenella, for lunch. At lunchtime I visited a 'remaindered' book sale and bought her a large, beautifully illustrated book on 'Butterflies and Moths of the British Isles'. Presented it to her when she came to see me at the end of the afternoon. As I've noticed before, she has an out-of-character but delightfully childlike joy when given a present. When she opened it she exclaimed with delight and kissed me on the lips. I said it would be too heavy to take with her on expeditions, but she said she had a very good visual memory and would be able to recall the images of rare species if she saw them.

On the following day she told him that she had planned with Fenella and their mutual friend, Samantha, to have a short holiday together in Cornwall at Easter. Samantha's aunt owned a holiday cottage in Polperro that they could use.

> *She remarked that her two friends were both hetero, but temporarily unattached – "so the holiday will be all about fresh air and exercise."*
>
> *I said, "I could lend you my old copy of 'Scouting for Boys', and that says a lot about fresh air and exercise." She laughed and said, "I'll definitely be taking your lovely little pocket guide to butterflies with me. I just hope there'll be some around at that time."*

The Easter holiday began on the Thursday of the following week. While Perdita was in Polperro with her friends Chatwell spent four days in Italy, based in Sorrento, and very briefly recording visits to Naples, Pompeii and Herculaneum. His return home on March 31st was the final entry in that volume of his diary, leaving a blank page and a half at the end. It was then I realized that there was now only one black-covered volume left unread.

I decided that I would make myself something to eat before I opened it.

26

My Saturday evening meal was a frugal one – cheese on toast, followed by a small tin of pears. When I had finished tidying up in the kitchen I went back to reading the final volume of Chatwell's diary.

He returned to work on the Tuesday after the Easter bank holiday, and again took small gifts of Italian chocolates for Sumintra and Perdita. The latter was late arriving, and put her head round his office door to apologise, saying she'd returned home very late the previous evening. When they finally got together over the post she proferred her cheeks to be kissed. He wrote:

> *She said the holiday had gone well – no*
> *arguments and a lot of laughs, even though they*
> *had had some rain. And she was feeling much*
> *more positive. Said it had been a bit early for*
> *butterflies, but she'd seen a few Whites and*
> *Fritillaries. Samantha had become interested*
> *because a couple of her sixth-formers were*
> *members of a local Butterfly Study Group, and she*
> *might decide to join it.*
>
> > *Saw her again at the end of the afternoon,*
> > *and we sat side by side as we talked. She'd been*
> > *thinking about sensuality, and why some people*
> > *have more of it than others. How much was*
> > *determined in childhood, she wondered. For a time*
> > *when her family was in Switzerland she'd been*
> > *looked after by a nursemaid who was the*
> > *daughter of Chinese refugees. Possibly because*
> > *her mother had been preoccupied elsewhere at the*
> > *time she'd become very attached to the girl. She*
> > *remembered lying on a bed with her and "feeling*

*her all over"; and she'd been really angry when
the girl left to get married.*

*As we talked I fondled her naked thigh under
her green corduroy skirt, and when my fingers
came to rest on her panty-covered mons veneris
they were allowed to gently rub. She stood up and
I raised her skirt at the back and kissed her
bottom repeatedly. Before she left I kissed her
cheeks and her neck, and as I'm writing this I can
still taste her perfume on my lips.*

On the following day he asked Perdita if she would like to take
advantage of a temporary lull in work activities by having
Thursday afternoon off and accompanying him on an outing to
Kew Gardens. He wrote: "She agreed very readily, and I
wondered if this might be the opportunity for which I have been
waiting." As I turned over the page I saw that his Thursday diary
entry was a long one. It began with comments on a 'Women's
Magazines Project' he was starting to plan.

*Perdita said dismissively that she never read
women's magazines, except in dentists' waiting-
rooms. I told her she should look at the statistics of
how many people were influenced by them.*

*The weather forecast isn't promising,
predicting that the bright spell we've been having
is about to end. However, Perdita said she'd like
to risk it, and seemed excited at the prospect. We
bought the ingredients of a picnic in Woolworth's
before taking the Tube to Kew Gardens.*

*Arrived there, we walked across the gardens
till we found a quiet spot behind the Temperate
House to eat our picnic – sausage rolls, a crusty
loaf with Bel Paese cheese, and slices of walnut
cake. We even had visits from a couple of
butterflies, a Large White and a Common Blue.*

Afterwards we walked around the lake. She was beginning to feel cold and I took off my raincoat and put it on her. Since I was wearing my leather jacket I didn't feel the cold – and anyhow I was too excited to notice it. Eventually found the way to Rhododendron Dell. I'd saved some walnut cake crumbs and fed a robin on my hand, then getting him to go on hers. We also saw a nuthatch, dunnocks and a greenfinch. After that we had a coffee, and then visited the herb garden at Kew Palace.

By this time a bank of black cloud was looming up, and we just reached the Tropical House when the rain began. Came to an illustration of the great double coconut, which looked very like a woman's bottom, and I fondled hers through the raincoat, prompting a laughing rebuke.

It was closing time and the rain was still quite brisk. So I slit the Woolworth's carrier bag down one side and she used it as a hat as we walked briskly back to Kew Gardens station, where we didn't have long to wait for a Tube. As we sat together she chatted animatedly about what we had seen, and in particular about the Tropical House.

For both of us Embankment was the interchange station, but as she stepped on to the escalator to the southbound Bakerloo I followed her. "You should have taken the northbound one," she said, glancing over her shoulder.

As we stepped on to platform level I asked, "Can I come home with you for a little while, and dry off?"

"No," she replied, smiling, as we walked together along the platform.

164

"You know you can trust me not to do anything you don't want me to do," I said.

"Yes, she replied, "but I also know that I can't trust myself. You're my mainstay, and if we got passionate and later on it went wrong, what would I do then? Or, if later I moved on to someone else, how would you feel?"

I replied that I was willing to take that risk. (It was a strange conversation to be having walking along a fairly crowded platform.) I wanted to give her pleasure, I said, and I was sure I could do it better than anyone else who had tried.

"I'm sure you would, but it's what might happen afterwards that bothers me," she said. And then the train arrived.

"This is getting to be like 'Brief Encounter'," I said. She laughed and kissed me lightly on the lips.

"I hope maybe one day you'll change your mind," I said as she boarded the crowded train. And feeling very like a character in a romantic film, I watched it pull away. Instead of going straight home I went back to the office, where now I am writing this and wondering what I should do next.

Next morning Perdita joined him as usual to go through the post. He wrote that,

When she entered the room I stood up at my desk and she came round it to kiss me on the cheek, saying, "I didn't thank you properly yesterday for the lovely afternoon you gave me." I returned her kiss with two, and went to sit at the table side by side while we looked at the post.

There weren't many items to deal with, and I then decided I ought to clarify yesterday's conversation. So I said, "When I wanted to go home with you yesterday I wasn't just wanting to have some more intimate fun together. If you'd been happy with how we got on – and I think you would have been – I would have asked you to marry me. You've said that what you want now is marriage, and you know that I'm in love with you."

She shook her head and said, "That was just what I was afraid of. If we'd gone to bed I know you would have been good, and I'd probably have fallen in love with you, and then I wouldn't have been able to say no. But it wouldn't have been right – for either of us."

"Do you think I'm too old for you?" I asked.

"No", she replied. "I think I prefer older men. The trouble is you know me so well, probably better than anyone else, and when I get married it has got to be to somebody who doesn't know me. If I'm going to make a success of marriage I've got to become a different person."

"I may know quite a lot about you," I said, "but I love what I know. And if you change I'll go on loving the new person that you make yourself. I've loved you through all the changes I've seen you making already."

"I know you have," she said, "and it's helped me to keep going. But we'd take everything you know about the past into the marriage and I want to leave it behind. Maybe I won't find anyone who'll have me, but if I do I'm going to make it work."

I decided there was no point in trying to change her mind. I've seen it change before, and if

I'm lucky I might be around when it changes again.

"You will. I'm sure of that," I said. "I'll go on hoping. And now I'm afraid I've got to have a meeting with Helen about the accounts. It's the end of the fiscal year and we've got to make sure they're all in order. Maybe we can have some time together before you go home this evening?"

She smilingly assented, and blew me a kiss as she was leaving. At about five o'clock she returned to my room, carrying cups of tea for us both. We drank it sitting side by side at the table, and she remarked that her back was a bit stiff, possibly because she'd got wet yesterday. I offered to massage it for her, and we both stood up.

I massaged through her light dress, under which she wasn't wearing anything, and before long I could feel her muscles relaxing. I moved round in front of her, kissed her cheeks and hugged her gently round the waist. I could feel her yielding to my embrace in a way that she's seldom done before, and so I pressed my advantage.

I put my hands under her dress and brought them up to stroke her naked back. She leant towards me, so that I could feel the warmth of her body, and in a moment we were simulating the rhythm of coitus – to my amazement and delight. When I fondled her breasts through the dress I was not surprised to find her nipples were already erect.

"How do I get to them?" I asked, and she laughed. I pulled down the elasticated top of the dress below her right breast and began to kiss and tongue the nipple. She uttered a little moan and I kissed her mouth. Once again she responded, and for several minutes we kissed

passionately while she stroked my back and responded to the rhythm. My hands strayed all over her silken skin and I talked in a low whisper, saying it was because I loved her that I wanted to make love to her.

Eventually my hand found its way inside her panties, caressing her mons veneris and stroking her pubic hair. She somehow indicated that she didn't want me to go further, even though her eyes were closed and her breathing had become shallow. She said, "You can feel how wet I am" – although actually I couldn't.

"Can I kiss your beautiful bottom?" I asked; and she laughed and said, "My pulchritudinous posterior?" And I replied, "That's what I had in mind."

I knelt down behind her and she held her dress up above her waist while I lowered her pink and white panties and covered those firm, silken-skinned buttocks with kisses, and one or two gentle bites. When I had kissed her all over her contours I pulled up her panties and took her in my arms for a final, passionate kiss on the lips.

She then had to leave because she is meeting Fenella for a meal at Il Portico this evening. When we parted in the street I took her hand and she gave mine a squeeze, saying, "See you on Monday." I went home feeling that hope might still be with me.

27

Eager to discover whether or not Chatwell's hope was illusory, I quickly scanned the few paragraphs of the Saturday and Sunday diary entries, and turned over to the entry for the following Monday. He wrote:

Up early and groomed myself with great care. On way to work bought two little bunches of fresias and put them on Perdita's desk. Now I must get some work done and try not to build my hopes too high. Will see if I can persuade her to take me home with her this evening.

After she'd arrived (a little late) I went into her office briefly. She smiled but seemed a little guarded. However, she didn't resist my kisses on the back of her neck, nor even the first touch of my hands on her breasts, although she did then gently remove them. She said she'd had a good weekend, and thanked me for the flowers. I said their sweet smell had made me think of her – even though she smelled more sweetly than ever they did.

About twelve she came to see me and said she'd like to go to Cranks for lunch. I offered to take her and she accepted. We had a vegetarian meal – pleasant if unexciting. Conversation wandered through books we'd read, childhood experiences and our mutual need sometimes to have time to spend alone.

When we got back to the office I said, "Why don't we both work very hard for a couple of hours and then you could take me home to play?"

Her reply was a very firm no. She'd given way to me yesterday, she said, but that was because of the mood she'd been in. She wasn't sure that she wanted to do that again.

At the end of the afternoon she brought me a cup of tea – but it's not tea and sympathy that I want now. I caressed her a little and she was slightly resistant, but accepted my kisses. At first we talked about trivialities. She said she was going to the launderette, and I asked her to think about what she could be doing instead. It wouldn't work, she said. Yesterday she got carried away, but she knew that in the long run she wanted to find someone who was different from me, and she didn't want to deceive me.

I could walk with her to the station, she said; and I did. She was going home to her parents' house to spend the evening and the night because it was her mother's birthday. My flowers this morning had reminded her that she ought to take some flowers, and she was going to buy them from a stall at the station. She said the girl who ran it was always very helpful; and she also settled for fresias. Departing, she held up her cheek to be kissed.

On the way home I felt despondent, but resolved not to give up.

Next morning Chatwell had to attend a meeting before going to the office. When he arrived there he looked in on Perdita. He wrote:

She smiled affectionately and said the evening had gone well. I kissed and hugged her and she didn't draw back. Said she was going to have lunch with her American friend, Fenella.

170

At the end of the afternoon she came to see me, and allowed me to stroke her back and fondle her thighs as we talked; but when my hands went to her breasts she gently removed them. Fenella had heard from their friend in Reading, Samantha, inviting them both to a meeting on Sunday of the 'Butterfly Study Group' which she has joined. Fenella had said she wasn't really interested, but Perdita thought she might go. She said the talk was to be about butterflies in New Zealand, which didn't particularly interest her, but she would be interested to find out what kind of group it was.

Then she speculated about whether she might try to write a book on butterflies for children. I suggested that she should check out whether any books of that kind already existed, possibly by chatting up an assistant in Foyle's children's department. If she started writing would I help her to keep at it, she asked; and I promised that I would.

We walked to the station together, and I kissed her goodbye quite tenderly.

In the remainder of the week there were no new developments. Each day Chatwell managed to have some intimate moments with Perdita, but she was always a little restrained. On the Friday, however, he wrote:

Perdita was bright and smiling, looking pretty in an old red-checked shirt and her celadon green jeans. I held her in my arms when she came to put a bag in my cupboard, and stroked her back and fondled her bottom. Then I lightly fondled her breasts, and that, too, was permitted.

At the end of the afternoon she brought me a cup of tea. We talked, and she told me about

171

having lunch yesterday with a 'New Scientist'
journalist who fancies her. She hadn't encouraged
him, she said, and thought he was a bit too
wrapped up in his work, and very self-assured.
When she was leaving I held her with my hands
on her soft hips and kissed her cheeks. Then I
fetched her bag from the cupboard. To my surprise
she put her arms around me and kissed me lightly
on the lips.

Monday brought new developments. Perdita had gone to the
Reading Butterfly Study Group and told him the outcome as soon
as they got together.

I immediately sensed a mood of excitement. She
kissed my cheek before she sat down, and said,
"The meeting was much more interesting than I
thought it would be. The speaker was a New
Zealander who's doing a course on lepidoptery at
Reading, but he already has a degree in farm
management. He's taken time off from running the
family farm with his father, growing kiwi fruit and
avocadoes. I thought it would probably be sheep
when I asked him what kind of farm it was. But
the interesting thing is that he's planning to start a
butterfly ranch when he goes home."

I said that sounded highly improbable, and
she agreed that that had been her own first
reaction. But apparently it's an idea that has
already been tried. It seems that there's a
butterfly house at Syon Park – which she wants to
visit – and a butterfly ranch for tropical varieties is
already being planned in Belize.

The speaker, whose name was Cyril
Campbell, had invited her and Samantha to have
a drink with him afterwards in the students' union

bar, and they had got on very well together. I asked what age he was and she said he must be over forty, because he'd mentioned seeing his father for the very first time when he'd returned in 1945 after serving in the army. "But he's quite youthful looking, because I expect he spends most of his time in the open air," she added. I got the impression that she likes him.

At the end of the afternoon she brought me a cup of tea and we sat side by side. I stroked her thigh as we talked, and once or twice she put her hand on top of mine. Before she left I kissed her and briefly fondled her bottom.

Next day the situation continued to develop. Perdita reported that she'd had a phonecall from Cy (the name by which he is known to his friends) and he'd invited her to go with him on Saturday to Syon House. She'd accepted; and when she'd suggested that he might like to spend the night at her flat, rather than travel back to Reading, he had "sounded surprised and delighted."

"I bet he was," I said, and she laughed. I was standing behind her chair, preparing to go to a meeting, and I kissed her cheek and then her neck. She turned her face up to me and I kissed her lightly on the lips.

On the following two days he had only brief encounters with Perdita, but they included kisses and fondling; and on Friday he invited her to have a lunchtime picnic with him.

We bought sandwiches, bananas and little chocolates, with orange juice, at the Italian delicatessen, and took them to our usual spot in St

*James's Park. Sat on the grass and Perdita pulled
up her skirt to expose her thighs to the sunshine.*

*The talk drifted to the past, and she told me
about her two teenage boyfriends, and also a girl
at school on whom she had a crush. On the way
back she mentioned Cy again, wondering what
she might give him to eat at the weekend.*

Once again Chatwell's weekend entries were minimal. One
sentence, however, revealed that he was seriously concerned about
Perdita's new relationship. He wrote: "This weekend could be a
turning-point, for she's likely to discover enough about Cy to
make up her mind about him." That observation came after he had
briefly recorded spending the afternoon in the Wallace Collection.
I turned to the Monday entry to discover whether he was right. He
wrote:

*Things never turn out as expected. Perdita smiled
hesitantly when I went into her room and stood by
her desk in the usual way. When I hugged and
kissed her she seemed quite welcoming, but she
wasn't talkative and I began to hope that the
weekend had not been a success.*

*A few minutes later she remarked that she'd
told her mother about Cy, and her mother hadn't
approved of him – "and she'd approve even less if
she knew his age." I said it was none of her
mother's business (and I think there might be a
tiny loophole there, but one that could also be
dangerous to me later on.)*

*In the afternoon she came to see me with
some work and we sat side by side. As we talked
I was allowed to hug her and put my hand down
inside her jeans to caress the tops of her buttocks.
Emboldened, I kissed her cheek and her neck.*

Eventually she said something like: "I'm not certain about the relationship with Cy. I have a feeling I'm much stronger than him in spite of his age. I could chew him up and spit him out if I wanted to." I responded, very carefully, that it might have something to do with his long years as a bachelor. She went on to say he had been "uncontrolled and quick to react to stimulus." (I wondered if that meant premature ejaculation, but I didn't ask.) It wasn't exactly a complaint, but it wasn't an enthusiastic endorsement, either. I felt cautiously heartened.

The conversation was warm and intimate, and all the while I continued to caress her. If this relationship with Cy (who actually hadn't expected to be sharing a bed with her) is not successful I think I might at last have a chance of winning her love. But she's still talking about visiting Cy next weekend.

When she was leaving she came willingly to be hugged, and I kissed her lightly on the lips.

In the remainder of that week Chatwell had some more moments of intimate physical contact with Perdita, but no more revealing conversations. On Friday she mentioned again that she would be going to Reading on the following day, but nothing more. Once more I turned with heightened curiosity to his Monday entry. He wrote:

Perdita arrived early at work and I went immediately to see her. She seemed relaxed and cheerful, and talked about having been allowed to cook for Cy and his Kiwi flat-mate, Bruce, on Sunday, to their apparent delight. She thought Bruce had been "mildly shocked" when he realized she was sharing Cy's bed. And she remarked that she'd had trouble getting to sleep, "but Cy seems able to sleep very easily." As we talked I kissed her cheek and fondled her thigh.

At lunchtime I went with her on a shopping expedition, having first bought sandwiches at the Italian shop and eaten them under the trees in Victoria Square. We then went to Woolworths, where she selected three pairs of panties (white with various coloured motifs) and I insisted on paying for them, saying, "I'm looking forward to seeing all three of them before long."

She laughed and said, "When the weather improves and I go back wearing dresses you'll probably have a chance." Had meeting in afternoon and didn't see her again before she left.

Glancing at the clock, I decided to have my bath and then take the diary to bed with me to discover what happened next.

28

Reading in bed was a favourite pursuit when I was a schoolboy, but in more recent years I have usually been ready to fall asleep as soon as my head hit the pillow. However, I had decided on an "early night" when I took the final volume of Winston Chatwell's diary to bed with me, to discover what happened next in the intriguing account of his relationship with Perdita Preston.

The weather was sunny on Tuesday, and once again they had a picnic together in St James' Park. They sat on the grass and watched a group of French schoolchildren, and a family of five young ducks. And he wrote:

Back in the office I kissed her tenderly before we went our separate ways. At the end of the afternoon she came to my office and we sat side by side, discussing the possibility of her writing a children's book on butterflies. I pulled up her sweater, opened a low button on her blouse and kissed her naked tummy. She remarked that she was short of blouses and I indicated that I would like to give her one.

I put my hand on her blouse-covered breast and when it was allowed to remain there I began to fondle gently. Soon she began to show signs of enjoyment and so I pulled up her sweater and inserted my fingers into her blouse. One of the buttons popped off, and I said that now I really would have to buy her another one.

I then undid a second button and got my lips to her breast, gently teasing the nipple, and immediately I felt her respond. So I took the whole breast into my mouth, caressing the nipple with my tongue. And then I transferred my lips to the other (left) breast, using my fingers to keep the first one stimulated. At one point I said, "I can't understand how anyone can use ugly names, like 'boobs', to describe these beautiful breasts."

A little later I discovered that I could use a sucking action with my lips to stimulate the whole of her breast while keeping my tongue on her nipple. She became very responsive, but eventually said, "You're exciting me too much." So I transferred my kisses to her neck and her cheeks, and eventually she persuaded me to button up her blouse. I was allowed to accompany her to the station.

For the remainder of that week Perdita, while remaining affectionate, avoided any more intimate encounters with Chatwell. On the Friday she mentioned casually that Cy was going to be visiting her again at the weekend, when they would be going together to the Zoo. On Saturday and Sunday Chatwell briefly recorded visiting the National Gallery and the Royal Academy, where he treated himself to tea in the Members' Room. On Monday, however, he tried again.

This morning asked Perdita if we could go at lunchtime to look for a blouse "to replace the one I ripped in my insatiable lust." She laughed, and asked if we could visit a stall in Covent Garden that Fenella had been telling her about. So that was where we went, and she found a white, lace-fronted one in her size, which was actually ridiculously cheap. Bought sandwiches on our way back and ate them at our desks.

At the end of the afternoon she came to see me. Earlier, when we'd been travelling together, she'd said that the weekend had been "all right", and she'd enjoyed the visit to the Zoo. I kissed her cheeks and neck, but when my hand approached her breast she said her breasts were feeling tender today – it might be because she'd had a bad period at the weekend. (I wonder if that might be the reason why there was no mention of night time activity in her weekend 'report'.)

So I asked, "Well, can I kiss your bottom, then?" and she replied, "All right, but just one." I rejoined, "I presume that means one on each delectable contour." She stood up and allowed me to raise her wine-coloured corduroy skirt above her waist as I knelt down behind her. I pulled down her blue silk panties and kissed each buttock in turn, and also gave each a gentle bite. But I then kept to her limit and replaced the panties and stood up.

She turned around and came to my arms while I covered her cheeks in kisses and my hands fondled her bottom. Having kissed all around her mouth, I asked, "Can I have one proper kiss?" She yielded her lips to me for one delicious kiss, but only for one, muttering something about not getting "too carried away".

I was allowed to accompany her to the station.

Next day Chatwell had his morning meeting with Perdita over the post, and she told him more about her weekend encounter with Cy.

"He has quite detailed plans for how he's going to set up the butterfly ranch," she said. "Where he lives is quite close to some beautiful beaches that are popular with holidaymakers, and he thinks they could easily be persuaded to pay for visiting the ranch. He even has plans to build a couple of holiday cottages for renting."

I asked whereabouts in New Zealand he lived and she said it was in Northland – which, it

179

seems, is the imaginatively-named most northerly district of North Island. He lives alone with his father, his mother having died two years ago; and his sister, Ella, got married a few years ago and lives with her husband, a transport engineer, in Auckland.

The evident interest she is taking in his circumstances disturbed me a little, even though earlier she had said that she thought she might be more 'highly sexed' than Cy is. She also complained that he seemed to want to spend every moment in the open air.

In the afternoon I had two meetings, and so I didn't have a chance to talk to her again today.

On Wednesday Chatwell was busy meeting people during most of the day, but at the end of the afternoon he was able to relax with Perdita. She showed him a newspaper article which cited some research into the importance for health of touching and being touched. He wrote:

I said that if scientific proof was needed I was sure that I'd be able to provide it. I'd often felt my skin responding her caresses. She agreed, and talked about having had experiences that confirmed the theory.

I then said it was time we provided a bit more evidence, and began to unbutton her multicoloured blouse, and she didn't try to stop me. I kissed each breast very tenderly, and then took each into my mouth in turn, teasing the nipples, which very quickly became erect, with my tongue. From time to time she gave little gasps of pleasure. I said how delightful it was that her breasts were exactly the right size to fit between my lips. Was it something she enjoyed, I asked; and she confirmed that it was. I said we must do it more often.

When it was time for her to leave I buttoned up her blouse and she came into a tight embrace while I kissed her lips and fondled her bottom. Walked with her to the station.

Thursday and Friday of that week were mainly occupied with the launch of the Women's Magazines Project (to which I remembered devoting an entire chapter in my book) and he had only brief contacts with Perdita. On Friday afternoon she told him that she would be visiting Reading at the weekend. It was going to be a long weekend because of the May Day bank holiday and the Tuesday which he had already decided to make an additional day off.

On Saturday Chatwell took off for Paris. His very brief diary entry noted that, on Sunday he "visited parts of the Louvre that I hadn't been to before." He also recorded spending time in the Quai d'Orsay and in several churches. On Wednesday morning he was back in the office, and saw Perdita to check the post, noting that:

She seemed to be in a cheerful mood. Her weekend had included a trip to the Cotswolds, and she said it had "gone well". As she sat beside me I fondled her naked thigh beneath her burgundy corduroy skirt. At lunchtime she had her hair trimmed. When in W H Smith's to buy a rubber I saw a beautiful book on Romanesque art in a sale they were having, and I bought it for her.

When she came to see me at the end of the day I gave her the book and it seemed to delight her. To my surprise and delight she kissed my cheek. Then she laughed and said she'd put lipstick on me, and started to rub it off with a tissue. I fondled her bottom through her skirt and,

admiring her new Liberty print blouse, gently
caressed her breasts a few times with my fingers.
Walked with her to the station, where she
proferred her cheek to be kissed.

Next day he noted that the weather was cooler, and that Perdita also seemed to be, just a little. He wrote:

It's not that she's unfriendly, but I can't feel any
physical openness to me. When she came to see
me in the afternoon I invited her to sit on my knee,
and she did, putting her arm firmly around my
shoulders. While we chatted I fondled her thighs
and planted occasional kisses on her cheek.

She mentioned that Cy was worried because
he and Bruce were going to have to leave their flat
in June because their lease will have run out.
Suddenly I saw the possibility of one last chance.
"Couldn't he come and live with you?" I asked.
"Then you'd both have a chance to get to know
each other better."

"Of course!" she exclaimed. "That's the
obvious solution. I'll talk to him on the phone
tonight." And she kissed me warmly on both
cheeks. When we stood up I took her in my arms
and, although she didn't resist my embrace, I felt
a certain reserve and so I didn't press too hard. I
was allowed to carry her bags to the station.

Next day Perdita told Chatwell that Cy had been very surprised, but delighted, by her suggestion, and would be moving in with her in June. Apparently he planned not to return home until August. She expressed concern about not wanting him to take over all the cooking, even though he was very competent. She said:

"He likes to cook elaborate meals that are very heavy, and takes ages over it." I suggested that she might draw up a rota. After all, it was her kitchen.

Once again she is going to spend Saturday and Sunday in Reading. Had only a short time with her today, but enjoyed a quick kiss and cuddle.

When they got together on the following Monday it was at the end of the afternoon. Perdita said she felt tired, having not slept well the previous night. Chatwell drew his chair close to hers and took her head on his shoulder.

She snuggled up, putting her arm around my neck. My free hand caressed her breast underneath her sweater and through her shirt, and she stayed there for more than five minutes. When we stood up I held her close and kissed her cheeks while I thrust my hand into the seat of her green striped trousers and fondled her bottom cheeks. She must have felt my mounting excitement but she stayed close and showed some signs of being stimulated. Eventually she said she had to go, and we walked together to the station.

29

It would normally have been time to switch out the light and go to sleep, but I was curious to know what Perdita finally decided and so I continued to read the final volume of the Chatwell diaries. On Thursday she asked if she could take the next week as a holiday. Cy had planned to visit Scotland, the country of his ancestors, before going home, and now he would like Perdita to accompany him. Needless to say, Chatwell agreed, remarking "I think the midges won't have started to bite yet."

On the Monday when she returned to the office after the holiday Chatwell wrote:

Perdita said she'd enjoyed the holiday, but it hadn't been wildly exciting, partly because the weather was very mixed. They'd started in Edinburgh, which she'd liked, and then moved to Inverary, to visit what Cy described as "Campbell country". She said, "I hadn't realized that all the Highlanders weren't on the side of Bonnie Prince Charlie. He told me the Campbells actually fought alongside the Government army at Culloden."

I said that myths were always less complicated than history.

At lunchtime we went to Victoria Square via the Italian shop, and had a picnic. The wind was cool, but intermittent sunshine warmed us up. We talked about a newspaper article she'd seen on how marriages in Russia often break up. Then she remarked that Cy seemed to be very untidy, adding "Not that I'm particularly tidy myself."

At the end of the afternoon we had only a short time together. I said, "Can I give you a little hug and then come with you to the station?" She came to my arms somewhat reluctantly, I thought, and when I kissed, hugged and fondled her

bottom she wasn't very responsive. At the station I
kissed her a hurried goodbye.

During the rest of the week he had some contact with Perdita every day, but on each occasion he commented that her response to his embraces had been "restrained" or "unenthusiastic". She had excused herself by saying she was having a difficult period, and he seemed to want to believe her. In the first week of June she was preoccupied with getting ready for Cy to move into her flat.

Chatwell then had a few days in the Netherlands, combining meetings with two editors and some holiday. He stayed in Haarlem overnight, enabling him to enjoy a candle-lit evening opening of the Frans Hals Museum. On the Friday he was back in the office and wrote:

Perdita seemed genuinely pleased to have me back. When we'd gone through the post I told her about the Dutch trip. As we sat together I stroked her thigh – in tight white trousers. She said that Cy had moved in with her on Wednesday. His flat- mate, Bruce, had rented a bed-sit in Battersea. Yesterday they had met together in a pub and Cy had been late for dinner – but she forgave him.

At the end of the day she came to see me again. I said, "It seems a long time since I gave you any proper kisses. Can I give you some now?"

Somewhat to my surprise she said, "Yes." I said, "I won't rip your blouse this time," and I carefully unbuttoned her green-checked shirt and quickly applied my lips to her left breast. When I'd kissed it all over I took it into my mouth and teased the now erect nipple with my tongue. Then I changed to the right breast and fondled the left with my hand.

Fully aroused now, my hand came round inside the front of her trousers, and her breathing quickened as I began to caress her mons veneris. Without much conviction she asked me to stop, and because I didn't want to risk losing the rest of our erotic contacts, I did. Instead, I held her very close to my body and she came willingly as I began gently to simulate the rhythm of coitus.

Then I turned her round and with fingers continually caressing both her naked breasts I pressed my rampant penis (through two constricting pairs of trousers) against the softness of her buttocks, thrusting rhythmically. Again, I felt her bottom responding to the rhythm.

After a few ecstatic minutes we were face to face and breast to breast again. Her hand was on the front of my trousers and I said, "Oh, please leave your hand there for just a minute. He's your most ardent admirer." And she did leave it there, stroking in an exploratory way, for maybe two minutes. Then she said, "We've really got to stop while we still can." And so we stopped. I walked with her to the station in companionable silence.

On the following Monday he noted that Perdita seemed to be worried about something and was unresponsive to his welcoming kiss. He wrote:

Then, to my surprise, she asked if we could have lunch together. Luckily I was free, and I suggested we go to the Capri, which is always a good place for a quiet chat. I had a busy morning, but at about one I went to her office and she was ready to come out.

While we were waiting for the first course to arrive she said, "Cy has proposed to me."

"Have you accepted?" I asked, and she nodded her head. Then, speaking very rapidly, as

she often did when she was nervous, she told me that they wanted to get married before he had to leave for home in early August, and so they needed to leave enough time for all the legal formalities involved in getting a licence. She had been checking on all the details, and it looked as if there wouldn't be a problem.

I said I was sure she had thought carefully about it, and I hoped that Cy had too. We ate our pasta in silence. Then, as Maria cleared the plates, she said she knew that she wasn't perfect herself, and she couldn't expect Cy to be either. I said that if anyone was looking for perfection they'd never get married – and that actually happened sometimes. And I added, "I'm fool enough to want him to be as good as he can be, for your sake."

She laid her hand on mine, very briefly, and gave a gentle squeeze. I asked what kind of wedding did she have in mind, and she said they wanted to do it very quietly in a registry office, without a lot of family involvement and with very few people. That would have the added value of keeping down the cost, I commented.

She said she would rather not tell colleagues at the office just yet. She wasn't in the mood for lots of congratulations. Maybe when her engagement ring was ready – Cy was having a 'family ring' altered to fit her - that might be a good time to make it known.

When we got back to her office and I was about to leave her and return to mine she snuggled against me and held me tightly. Planted passionate kisses on her cheeks and her neck, and fondled her bottom. She said Cy would be meeting her at the station to do some shopping before they went home, and so I needn't accompany her at the end of the afternoon.

On the Wednesday Perdita had another conversation with him about future plans. He wrote:

When we had finished going through the post Perdita told me that Cy had heard from his sister, Ella. She and her husband, Shane, were going to come to London for the wedding and then have a touring holiday in Europe before returning to New Zealand. I made reassuring noises about it being good for him to have someone from his family at the ceremony.

Kissed and hugged her lightly before she returned to her own office. Had meeting at the IoJ and so didn't see her again in the afternoon.

Next day she told Chatwell that a date had been decided for the wedding. It would be on August 9, and they were then going to leave straight away for New Zealand, but would stop off for a week's honeymoon in Thailand on the way. He wrote:

Before she left my office I kissed her hands and hugged her tightly, several times touching her breast, but only lightly. And she seemed happy when I kissed her cheeks. She asked to have tomorrow off "to deal with lots of paperwork on a day when officials are in their offices," and of course I agreed.

Chatwell had arranged to take the following week as holiday. He spent it in Venice, visiting Padua, Murano and Burano, and viewing innumerable pictures in galleries and churches. His return flight, he noted, was "exceptionally good". Back in the office on Monday morning, Perdita came to see him as usual. He wrote:

She was interested to hear about the holiday, and recalled memories of places she'd visited when she was studying in Perugia. Then she expressed a slight concern about Cy liking to spend time in the pub with Bruce. I made reassuring noises. When she got up to return to her office I kissed her cheek, and to my surprise and delight she kissed me lightly on the lips.

She had mentioned, jokingly, that while she'd bought two new dresses she really should have been replacing her panties. So at lunchtime in Woolworth's, I bought her a pack of four pairs of panties – blue, white, yellow and pink. I put them in a large envelope with a note saying, "We must get to the bottom of this," and left it on her desk.

When she came to see me at the end of the day she thanked me, laughing at the joke. Later, when she stood up to leave, I hoisted her skirt at the back and put my hand into her panties to fondle the smooth, cool flesh of her bottom. Once again she surprised me by kissing me on the lips.

We left together, and I said, "I think I'd better not kiss you at the station from now on. I wouldn't mind if people made comments about me, but I wouldn't want any comments to be made about you." She gave me a hug, which I think signified gratitude. I carried her bags to the station and we parted with smiles, but no kisses.

30

I glanced at the clock on my bedside cabinet. It would normally have been time to go to sleep, but I was intrigued to discover how Perdita resolved her apparently conflicting desires – if she did. She reminded me just a little of my favourite historical heroine, Catherine the Great. So I went on reading.

On Tuesday Chatwell wrote that when he saw Perdita in the morning she was upset because some of their travel arrangements were going to have to be altered.

I took her in my arms and held her while we talked – and she held me tightly. Kissed her gently and she seemed to become less unhappy about the changes. We were almost interrupted by Sumintra, but luckily we heard her approaching.

At lunchtime we bought a picnic in the Italian shop and took it to the Park. Chatted mainly about books we had read in our childhood. She was surprised that mine had included Rider Haggard and G A Henty, and I was surprised that she hadn't read 'War and Peace'.

When she came at the end of the afternoon she was complaining of a headache. I stood behind her and massaged gently, running my fingers over her scalp. We talked about her problems of deciding what to take with her to New Zealand.

The headache lifted and I kissed her cheek. I put a hand on her breast but she removed it, gently but firmly. However, when I asked if I could kiss her bottom she agreed, and stood up while I hoisted her skirt and lowered her panties. I kissed very comprehensively, and took each buttock gently between my teeth. But she resisted any more intimate caresses, and then it was time for her to leave.

Next day, the beginning of July, he saw Perdita briefly in the morning but had interviews all afternoon, and she had already left when they were finished. On the Friday he wrote in the diary (presumably soon after sitting down at his desk) that he was feeling optimistic.

Will she still be receptive today, I wonder. I'll not be able to see her until later in the morning.

Saw her briefly before lunchtime, when she didn't turn away from my kisses. In the afternoon she came to see me earlier than usual, at about 5.20, saying she'd come earlier than usual because she wanted to leave earlier, to meet her mother.

We sat side by side and talked about the coming weekend. I put my hand under her green corduroy skirt and stroked her naked thigh; and then I touched her breast and said, "It seems a long time since these little beauties had the kisses they deserve. Can I give them some now?"

To my delight, and slight surprise, she said "All right".

Immediately I began to unbutton her multi-striped blouse, and my fingers quickly found the softness of her breasts. Then my lips went to work on her right breast, kissing all round the nipple before coming to rest on it. After that I took the whole breast between my lips and teased the firmly erect nipple with my tongue. It was then the turn of her left breast, while my fingers kept the right one in harmony.

As I kissed and caressed she said, "Nobody has ever done this as well as you do. Maybe it's because they've been thinking mainly about their own orgasms. You never seem to want to stop."

I replied, "I would want to stop only if I was being allowed to move to what comes next."

She said she supposed it was mainly about levels of sensuality, and added, "But I think sometimes it's also about feeling embarrassed. You don't embarrass easily." We both laughed. I continued to kiss and caress, and she began to show signs of excitement, her breathing becoming quicker and shallower. I used one hand to raise her skirt at the front and then began to stroke and caress the tops of her thighs and her groin. When she made no protest I went under the edge of her panties until I felt her pubic hair. I then began very gently to massage, and I could feel her body responding to my rhythm. My own excitement was mounting rapidly, but suddenly – I think she had become alarmed by her own degree of involvement – she said, "Oh Winston, we've got to stop. We mustn't get carried away."

I said, "I can never refuse you, because I love you"; and I began to disengage. She said she was feeling very hot, and so I fetched her a glass of water, and persuaded her to sit on my knee while she drank it. Her mother had wanted to come and help her choose some things, she said, and she thought it would be kind to let her do that. Now she was feeling a little anxious because she thought their tastes would probably not coincide. I said that being kind, now that she was on the verge of going away, was more important than getting the choice of a dress exactly right.

Then it was time for her to leave; and she came to my arms to be kissed before we parted at the front door.

On the following Monday morning Chatwell noted that when Perdita came to go through the post with him he immediately asked her how the shopping expedition had gone, and she said it had gone surprisingly well. But he thought she was looking tense.

I soon discovered the reason. When we had finished doing the post she said, "I'd like to change my hours please. I want to revert to coming in early and leaving at five."

Immediately I guessed the significance of what she was saying. "Does that mean you want to stop having time alone with me in the afternoon?" I asked.

She nodded her head and said, "Now that I'm really getting married I've got to be more careful about what I do. I would blame myself if somebody said something that put a doubt in Cy's mind." Maybe it was because of her continuing doubt about her own self-worth that she was so afraid of losing him, she went on. She still couldn't believe that anyone would want to marry her. She had to stop now doing anything that might affect her marriage.

I realized that what I had so long dreaded had actually happened. Our intimate relationship was over. To my surprise and annoyance I felt tears welling up in my eyes. Clearly it also took her by surprise, and she exclaimed in a tone of real concern, "Oh, Winston, I didn't know it meant so much to you."

"Nothing else means anything to me," I replied, as I struggled without success to hold

back the tears. (Looking back now, I wonder whether they had flowed after so many years of continence because the memory of another loss had been triggered.) "Don't pay any attention to me," I went on. "I'm just being stupid."

She began to cry, too, and I said, "Oh, I didn't want to upset you" – and I meant it. I went on, "You must do what you think is best; and if you need any help I'll still be here. But because I love you I hope you won't need me."

She held out her arms to me as I continued crying. I think it's the first time she's ever done that. I moved towards her and we came together in a passionate, mutually comforting embrace. For a few minutes we clung together. Then it was time for her to leave. I said again, "You must do what you think best." I opened the door for her, kissed her cheek and gave that beautiful bottom a valedictory pat.

I remained behind to write up this diary entry while the events are still fresh in my mind. It will probably be the last entry that will have any interest for me in years to come.

At least I once again have the ability to weep.

During the rest of that week his entries were shorter, but he still recorded meeting Perdita in the mornings, and there was a restrained affection between them. Chaste kisses on the cheek seemed to be the order of the day. On the Tuesday he commented, "I thought her eyes looked unhappy, in spite of an occasionally smiling mouth." Next day he wrote, "Had a brief business meeting with Perdita in her room, standing facing her across the desk. We talked naturally enough." On Friday he wrote, "I asked if she was doing anything special at the weekend, and she replied, 'Just the usual'. That, for me, was the end of a miserable week."

Chatwell had planned a short visit to Barcelona in the following week to meet a regional newspaper editor, and he seems to have decided to extend it to fill the entire week. He commented that the editor appeared to see an exchange visit as "an opportunity to spread Catalan nationalist propaganda." He appears to have used the last three days of the trip as a kind of homage to George Orwell, with visits to Saragossa and Huesca.

Back in the office on Monday, Perdita proferred her cheek for a kiss when she came to see him, and wanted to talk about some of the minor problems involved in arranging the wedding. She asked if the following day would be appropriate for telling colleagues about her intentions, and he agreed to arrange a staff meeting in the morning.

All four of their colleagues were present next morning, and Chatwell immediately told them the purpose of the meeting. Perdita shyly exhibited her engagement ring, a single ruby set in platinum, and there was general surprise at the imminence of her departure. He noted that Sumintra appeared to be really saddened by the news; and afterwards Perdita told him that the two of them had had a lot of intimate chats over the years. In the afternoon he asked Sumintra if she would like to arrange the collection for a staff wedding present and she readily agreed.

On the following day he wrote:

When Perdita came to see me this morning I said to her, "Although I would very much like to give you something really valuable as my personal wedding gift I think that might be embarrassing for you." She nodded, and I went on, "Is there anything unostentatious that you would like to have?" She asked me to give her a day or two to think about it; and I asked her to talk to Sumintra about what she might like to have from colleagues collectively.

She came to me for a kiss on the cheek when she was leaving.

On Thursday Perdita asked if she could take the next week off to make preparations for travelling, and wind things up at home. After that, she said, she would like to stay at work until the day before the wedding – a Saturday. Chatwell agreed, but wrote that he was surprised she'd wanted to keep working until the last minute. He noted that he had no plans to replace her, and would make more use of the agency which already provided translators of languages such as Dutch and Danish when required.

The daily entries were becoming briefer and briefer. In the week when Perdita was on leave Chatwell recorded little more than the names of people with whom he had meetings or correspondence. When Perdita returned on the following Monday he wrote:

> *When Perdita came to see me I kissed her cheek and complimented her on a new blouse she was wearing. She said it was really part of her 'trousseau'. Bright-eyed and vivacious, she talked a bit about the wedding arrangements, which are very simple.*

Next day they weren't able to get together, except very briefly, until the end of the afternoon.

> *Perdita asked me if I would accompany her to the Oxford Street Marks and Spencer on the Number Two bus, and we had a chance to chat on the journey. Her plans seem to be working out well. I left her at the side door while she went round to the main entrance to meet Cy. He was going to visit the gents' outfitting department. I bought a couple of items in the food store before walking home.*

On Wednesday she asked Chatwell if the presentation of the staff wedding gift could take place next day, "and can you keep it brief please? I don't want to get emotional." He agreed, and on Thursday the staff meeting duly took place. He wrote:

> *Before the staff meeting I went to her office and gave her the leather-bound photo album she'd suggested as my personal gift – wrapped up for me by the helpful assistant at John Lewis. I kissed her lightly on the cheek; but when she opened it she threw her arms around my neck and kissed me firmly on both cheeks. I said, "It's time we went to meet the others."*
>
> *At the staff meeting I made a brief, conventional little speech about how much Perdita had contributed to the setting up of JEEP, and how sadly she would be missed by everyone. She took with her the good wishes of us all. And then Sumintra presented her with the gift, a set of table mats decorated with pictures of London, supplemented by a silver cake-slice, because the contributions had been so generous. I claimed the privilege of kissing the bride, and planted a chaste little kiss on her cheek to colleagues' applause.*
>
> *That afternoon I helped her carry the gifts to the station, and she asked if I would help her again tomorrow, because she still had some items to clear from her office, and she would be picking up her bouquet from the friendly girl at the station flower stall. I agreed.*

On Friday morning Chatwell was surprised when Perdita asked him if they could have a picnic lunch together in the Park. He wrote:

We followed the familiar procedure, buying sandwiches and a couple of little cakes in the Italian shop. For a short time we were able to sit in sunshine while we ate, but then the sky clouded over and it began to rain. As we walked quickly back I took off my jacket and draped it over her shoulders to cover her multi-coloured striped blouse. I said, "It's not the first time I've had to do that"; she laughed and said, "Oh yes, I remember."

At the end of the afternoon I walked with her to the station, carrying her heavy bag, which I held while she went to the flower stall and returned carrying a tasteful little bouquet.

"I can manage the bag now," she said. "I'll balance the flowers on top."

I handed over the bag, but took the bouquet from her, saying, "Send me a card when you have your first baby", and adding, "I'll carry the flowers to the ticket barrier".

When we got there I gave her the bouquet and she leant forward and kissed me lightly on the lips. If I should forget every other kiss I've ever been given, that is a kiss I will always remember. Then she was gone.

There is nothing more to be said.

The remainder of the page was blank, but I noticed there was something underneath the empty facing page. Turning it over, I discovered the photograph of an attractive young woman, holding a tiny baby on each arm. The photo was fastened lightly at each corner by a small blob of Blutak. I detached it and turned it over, to see a message on the back.

Dear Winston

Isabella is on my right arm and Edward on my left. The butterfly ranch is up and fluttering, and we are very happy. I hope you are, too.

Love, Perdita

I slipped the photograph back into the diary and laid it on top of the bedside cabinet. Thinking about ways in which I might be able to dispose of the diaries, I switched off the lamp; and very quickly I fell asleep.

31

After showering and shaving I had a leisurely breakfast, and decided that I needed to take some exercise. On an impulse I went by Tube to Westminster and walked through St James's Park, hoping I could identify the location of Chatwell and Perdita's favourite picnic place. Because I had been to the former premises of JEEP I guessed the direction they would have taken to arrive there, and so I was able to work out where they would probably have sat. I don't think the lay-out of the park has changed very much over the past thirty-three years.

Content with my discovery, I walked through the Green Park to the Jubilee line station of that name and took the Tube back to Marylebone. In the station Marks and Spencer I bought a salmon and cucumber sandwich and an apple for my lunch.

In the afternoon I turned on the television to watch England play Pakistan in a one-day cricket international. They looked as if they were heading for a win when the telephone rang. For a moment I hesitated, but luckily I decided to answer. The caller was Judith, just arrived back in London.

I remembered to ask first about her mother's health, and having heard she'd made a good recovery, I expressed pleasure at hearing her voice once again. After a couple of minutes of inconsequential chat she said, a little hesitantly, "Before I had to rush away unexpectedly, you suggested I might come round for a meal one evening. Is the invitation still on?"

Surprised and delighted, I stammered, "Of course it is. When might you be able to come?"

"What about tomorrow evening?" she replied.

I instantly agreed, and arranged that I would meet her in Portland Place at five-thirty, and walk here with her if she felt like stretching her legs after a day in the office – a suggestion she seemed to like. And then I asked, "Is Wiener Schnitzel something you would be happy with as a main course?"

"It's one of my favourites," she replied. "I look forward to seeing how you perform in the kitchen – and of course I'll be happy to help. By the way, have you finished reading those mysterious diaries yet?"

"I have," I replied, "and I'll tell you about them if you're interested. But I don't think I'll be telling anyone else."

Other novels by Derek Walker

(distribution at www.lulu.com and www.amazon.co.uk)

THE PEACEKEEPERS TRILOGY

Three novels which follow the fortunes of a group of friends, and their children, against the background of public events in the changing world, from 1937 to 1991. Details of the individual volumes below:-

SLEEP QUIETLY IN YOUR BEDS

When Daniel retrieves the scarf dropped by Ruth at a 1937 peace rally he quickly gets to know her and her friend Nancy; and before long he introduces them to Arthur, who like himself is a postgraduate student at the London School of Economics. They are all idealistically committed to activities that they hope will prevent another war in Europe. And since they are all unattached, the prospect of more intimate relationships very soon begins to influence their attitudes to one another. In the months that follow their circle of friendship begins to widen. Roddy, a student days friend of Daniel, returns from the Spanish Civil War; Freddie, a young aristocrat, joins them in a radical political project; and Margarita, a refugee from Spain, attracts their sympathetic support. As their private lives become more complex public events begin to intrude, with dramatic consequences. But Mr Chamberlain flies to Munich and returns to tell them they can now sleep quietly in their beds.

DON'T LOSE IT AGAIN

Daniel, Ruth, Arthur, Nancy and Margarita have survived the Second World War and are determined, in their different ways, to play a part in preventing such a catastrophe from ever happening again. Almost by accident Arthur becomes an MP in 1945. To Daniel's satisfaction the Army assigns him a job preparing for the new United Nations Organization. Ruth, who trained as a teacher of German, has an idea for a novel that will remind its readers of the different Germany that existed before the years of the Kaiser and Hitler. All are impatient to return to 'normality' in their private lives. However, as in the years before 1939, it is public events in distant places that determine how their lives develop. The action moves between London, New York, Switzerland and Paris in ways that they couldn't have predicted.

SEND NOT TO KNOW

The Cold War is coming to an end, as the Soviet Union holds free elections and the Berlin Wall is breached. Dan Leyland (son of Arthur and Ruth) is chairing a conference of European NGOs in Perguia and observes that some colleagues are unhappy about having their political illusions shattered. An Italian contessa who is acting as an interpreter confides in him about her troubled marriage, and he glimpses a possibility of ending his own post-marital loneliness. Returned home, Dan talks with his parents and their friends about their hopes and fears for the 21st Century. The action moves from London to Switzerland, to a hospital ward, and then to Germany and Italy. It culminates in a change of fortune for Dan when he least expects it.

The Alternative Worlds Trilogy

Three novels set in the 18th, 20th and late 19th Centuries which assume that history could have produced very different outcomes. Details of the individual volumes below:-

A CASUAL CONQUEST

A young man from Japan starts his first job with the Honourable West Europa Company in Antwerp – in an 'alternative history' scenario in which Eighteenth Century Europe, having earlier been devastated by Mongol and Ottoman invasions, is reminiscent of South Asia in the dying years of the Mughal Empire. Before long he is listening to the Mozart Minstrels and is seduced by the Duchess of Holstein (who in 'real time' would have been

Catherine the Great). Visiting Britain he sees a new altarpiece painted by Gainsborough and helps a young nun to escape to Antwerp. His bosses debate whether a trading company should take responsibility for governing failed states, and send him to observe a war in northern Germany between ambitious local rulers. He meets a famous native philosopher called 'Voltaire', and wonders if the British girl he left behind in Antwerp will welcome his return.

MISRULE BRITANNIA

A journalist sent to cover a civil war in a former colony is plunged into the conflicts and corruption of an underdeveloped country. While the war escalates he falls in love with the woman of mixed race assigned to be his photographer. And when he gets close to the charismatic rebel leader he sees how personality can influence politics. The story sounds familiar, but the ex-colony is Britain and the journalist is Japanese – in an 'alternative history' scenario where eastern Asia takes on the historical role of western Europe. Looking at a world stage on which the actors have changed costumes may give the reader a new perspective on real events in recent decades. The pains and pleasures of the individual characters, however, could happen at any time, in any place.

MANIFEST DESTINY

A group of archaeologists from the United Provinces of Zanulikaz (which consists of most of Western Europe) take part in a 'dig' in the island which in the 'real world' is called Crete. They hope to find evidence of why the continent of Eurasia failed to develop an advanced civilization before it was occupied by colonisers from technologically superior nations in North America. A series of events take place that are strongly reminiscent of events in the 'real world' at the beginning of the 20th Century. They make startling discoveries, encounter revolution and war, and meet people very similar to those who were living in the 'real world' a century ago.

Other Novels

FOND DELUSIONS

In his final year at grammar school in Northern Ireland David Hunter's ambition is to work for peace in a world where the hydrogen bomb has just been invented. He wins a scholarship to the London School of Economics, and falls in love with a beautiful classmate. But when his love affair fails he joins the Foreign Legion, and takes part in the invasion of Suez. Returning injured to London he has an unexpected encounter that gives him new hope and a better understanding of the past.

SENSE AND SENSUALITY

When Fatima, an asylum-seeker from Kazakhstan, meets Duncan Crauford she asks him to give her a bird's eye view of the history of Western civilization, to help her become British. Their quest takes them to the British Museum, the National Gallery and other sources of 'visual aids' in London. Meanwhile, Duncan, who is secretary-general of an international think-tank, is working with Paula, a Ugandan academic, on an analysis of the UN's failure to prevent genocide in Darfur. And his erotic friendship with Helen, a sensual university lecturer, is continuing even though she has decided to look for a husband, and thinks he isn't husband material. Her rejection makes him realize that he, too, is urgently in need of someone to share his bed; but he wonders what kind of woman could possibly be interested in a battle-scarred veteran like himself.

FAKING NEWS

When a minor news item on Radio 4 prompts Adam Turnbull to phone a friend he unwittingly takes the first step towards involvement in an international crisis. The action takes place a few years into the future, but underlying trends in politics and the media show few signs of change. Adam, an academic specialist in Balkan Studies, is sucked into ethnic cleansing, kidnapping and diplomatic deception, and he witnesses ways in which political, religious and NGO groups manipulate the media and are manipulated by them. His unwitting involvement in public events also brings him into intimate contact with two attractive women.

All Derek Walker's novels are available by 'Print on Demand' from www.lulu.com and www.amazon.co.uk